D0341214

Night Wings

Also by

JOSEPH BRUCHAC

Skeleton Man
The Return of Skeleton Man
Whisper in the Dark
The Dark Pond
Bearwalker

Night Wings

JOSEPH BRUCHAC

Illustrations by
Sally Wern Comport

HarperCollins*Publishers*

Library of Congress Cataloging-in-Publication Data

Bruchac, Joseph, date.

Night wings / Joseph Bruchac ; illustrations by Sally Wern Comport. —1st ed.

p.   cm.

Summary: After being taken captive by a band of treasure seekers, thirteen-year-old Paul and his Abenaki grandfather must face a legendary Native American monster at the top of Mount Washington.

ISBN 978-0-06-112318-4 (trade bdg.)

ISBN 978-0-06-112319-1 (lib. bdg.)

1. Abenaki Indians—Fiction. [1. Abenaki Indians—Fiction. 2. Indians of North America—Northeastern States—Fiction. 3. Monsters—Fiction. 4. Washington, Mount (N.H.)—Fiction.] I. Comport, Sally Wern, ill.   II. Title.

PZ7.B82816Ni 2009	2008032096
[Fic]—dc22	CIP
	AC

Typography by Ray Shappell

09   10   11   12   13   CG/RRDB   10   9   8   7   6   5   4   3   2   1

❖

First Edition

For my grandchildren,
Carolyn Rose and Jacob Bowman.
May our stories always give you strength.

It would not have been possible for me
to write this story (and many others)
without the generous guidance I was given
over the years by Abenaki elders and
tradition bearers Maurice Dennis/Mdawelasis
and Stephen Laurent/Atian Lolo.

Their gifts of story will not be forgotten.
Their feet are now on the road of stars,
but their voices will always be with us.

Contents

Night Wings

Prologue

It's quiet outside. Too quiet. No crickets, no scrabble of shrews and mice in the grass, not even an owl calling. This kind of quiet is ominous. But I want to believe it might be safe. That I might survive the night.

Here inside this cave there are sounds. There's the drip of water from the ceiling, where ancient water from some spring within the heart of the mountain has seeped through. Bat wings flutter softly in the deeper darkness behind me.

I think I hear something out there. It's a faint sound like the flap of wind against canvas. It's the sound of wings, of something in flight that shouldn't be real. Something that should just be a fantasy.

But fantasies don't have claws. I force myself not to reach and feel the place where my jacket was torn on my left shoulder. It aches there, but touching it will make it worse.

I look outside. Maybe I just imagined that sound. It's nearly midnight, two hours since I took refuge in this narrow cave. I can see the wide expanse of sky in front of me, the shapes of other slopes against the horizon. No lights, though, aside from the stars.

Suddenly something drops down with a whomp of wings that blot out the stars. Two red eyes stare at me from the inhuman face of the one who guards this place. The one who will not rest until it has me in its fierce grasp.

CHAPTER ONE

Family Tradition

I've always loved watching birds, the way they spread their wide wings, going up and up until they are out of sight. I've always thought about what it would be like to fly with a flock of geese or catch a thermal and soar next to a golden eagle. I can't imagine anything that would be cooler than that. I feel—or at least I used to feel—so close to those wide-winged fliers.

I also sort of look like a big bird. I have a narrow face, big eyes, and one of those classic northeastern-Indian noses. A beak. Plus my hair, which I keep in a sort of combination brush cut and Mohawk, rises up like a heron's crest. I'm so tall and thin that I towered over everybody else at West End Junior High. And although my legs are skinny, they have a lot of spring in them. I was the best high jumper there. My track coach, Mr. Dunkle, told me that when I went over the bar, it looked as if I was in flight. I liked that.

Poor Mr. Dunkle, who was also the basketball coach, looked like he was about to cry when I told him I was leaving at the end of last school year. Despite the fact that I had already told him I wasn't interested in playing, he'd been hoping to convince me to try out for the basketball team. He saw me as his new star center. Ha! As if someone who trips over his own feet when he tries to run and bounce a basketball at the same time could ever take to the court with any success. When it comes to team sports, I'm about as graceful and coordinated as a crippled duck. The reason I do so well at high jump is that it's just me out there. Plus it ends with falling on your back. That is something I know I'm good at. Coach Dunkle said that I wasn't really clumsy, that I was just getting used to my size and that I was self-conscious. But there was still no way that I was going to pick up b-ball.

"Honey," a voice calls from the next room of the trailer.

"Yeah, Mom?"

"Are you sure you are going to be all right here with your grampa?" Her voice is anxious.

I look around the little room that is going to be mine for at least the next school year. *If I liked living in a closet,* I think, *I'd be happy as a bug in a rug.* But I don't say that. How can you be sarcastic when your mom is being deployed to a war zone in the Middle East?

"Yeah," I say, raising my voice to a high-pitched, childish tone. "I'll be peachy keen!"

Mission accomplished. It makes her laugh. But it's a brief laugh. "Are you absolutely sure?" she asks. She pokes her head in through the doorway to look down at me, sitting on my bed, which is so low to the ground that my knees are around my shoulders. "Can you be honest, Pauley?"

I raise my hands and hold them out so that they almost touch the two walls on either side. I not only raise my voice, I make it shaky to the point of panic.

"Considering my severe claustrophobia, how could I not be happy here?"

This time Mom laughs so hard she has to sit down on the bed next to me. She leans her head on my bony shoulder and hugs me. She's still laughing some, but her eyes are glistening and I know she's having a tough time keeping back the tears.

"Pauley," she whispers, "you are so much like your father." She gives me one more squeeze, stopping just short of cracking my ribs. Mom is strong, almost scarily so. I guess it's because her people are Bear clan, descended from real bears—at least according to one of our tribe's stories! Dad's people are Fortunes—Water people—which doesn't explain why both he and I are built like anorexic basketball players.

"Will he be there when you get off the plane?" I ask.

Dad was deployed a year ago. We talk to him a lot over the phone and even see him sometimes—but only on our computer screen in shaky videos when he is allowed to send them.

"He better be," she replies.

There's a real smile on her face this time. Her unit is going to be at the same base as his, and they'll be able to spend a lot of time together. According to Dad, what they have most over there is free time and boredom—punctuated by moments of absolute chaos and screaming terror.

"Just think," she says, and I know what she's about to say because it's an old worn-out joke in our family, one I have even heard Grampa Peter crack, "both of your parents are going to be 'soldiers of fortune.'"

I laugh because I am supposed to laugh. Sure, I'm glad they will be together. I am also scared to death that I'll never see either of them again in the flesh.

"I wish I could go with you," I say.

Mom punches me in the arm. "No, you don't," she says. "And there is no way your father and I are ever going to give you permission to enlist before you turn eighteen. If I have my way, you're going to college first. You have your own wars to fight here."

Just four or five more years, I think. I'm thirteen now. And there's a long tradition of military service on both sides of our family. Grampa Peter's war was Vietnam, where he earned a Bronze Star and three Purple Hearts. Great-grampa Sam and Great-grampa Nicol both died on Iwo Jima. And it goes back like that all the way to the American Revolution, where no less than a dozen of my ancestors served on the side of the colonies after our people swore they would no longer fight against this country. They and their descendants would be connected to the defense of America as tightly as the links of an iron chain. I'm not going to be the one to break that chain.

Someone claps his hands together lightly outside the door. It's Grampa Peter using the old, polite way of announcing his presence.

"Okay, Tongwes," Mom says, using the old Abenaki word for "Father" as she always does when she speaks to him. Even though Grampa Peter is my dad's father, it's her way of showing him respect. "I'm ready."

I sense rather than hear Grampa Peter going back into the living room, where Mom has her bags. Grampa can pretty much make himself undetectable, which is why he did so well as a scout in Vietnam. But I can almost always sense when he's near, even when he's creeping up from behind in the stalking game he's played with me ever since I was two years old.

Grampa Peter is also what you'd call—if you were into understatement—a man of few words. He seldom utters more than two or three at a time. But he can say more with a gesture or an expression on his face than most people can in a ten-minute speech. Like when he raises an eyebrow. That is his way of gently suggesting that you need to rethink whatever you just said or did because you've got it wrong.

Mom stands up and straightens her uniform coat. We're driving her to the bus that she and the others in her Guard company will be taking to Boston, where they'll fly out from Logan Airport. So our good-byes are going to be sooner rather than later. Not that we say good-bye. What we say is *olipamkaani*. Good travels.

Mom turns around and hugs me again. She holds on for a long time and I let her. I don't want her to go, but I would never say that. Finally, though, I pretend to take a strangled breath.

"Lungs crushed," I croak. "Need to breathe."

Mom laughs. Even though I know she is doing it because she knows I want to make her laugh, I laugh with her. Then she goes out the door and I follow. There's nothing more I can tell her now. I have to let her focus on going, and on taking care of herself while she is gone.

So I don't say a word to her about the dream I had last night.

CHAPTER TWO

Making It Through

Grampa Peter and I don't wave as Mom steps onto the bus. We just walk to the truck without looking back over our shoulders. It's an old tradition in our family that whenever someone has to go off to war, you don't make a big deal about it. No weeping or carrying on like the little boy back at the curb, whose volume is going up so high that he's splitting our eardrums.

"I don't want Daddy to go, Mommy. No! Noooo! I don't want him to go! I want my daddy!"

To be honest, there's a part of me that wants to do just what he's doing. But that won't change anything. There's nothing I can do to stop my mom from going away. I can only try to make

that parting easier for her. Our elders always say that when a man—or a woman these days—leaves to defend the people, his or her mind must be focused on the task ahead. If your loved ones are trying to pull you back with theatrics and pleading words, it may make you feel guilty about leaving them. Feeling guilty about leaving your family can make you lose focus, and that's the worst way to be when you are going into danger. When your life is threatened, you've got to stay calm and keep a clear head.

That's how Grampa Peter made it through Vietnam during the Tet Offensive. When other men were running around like chickens with their heads cut off, he kept his gun locked and loaded and made sure his company kept their perimeter secured. And the calm image of his family he carried in his head kept him cool.

"Weren't you scared when they were coming through the wire in the darkness?" I asked him once.

"Sure," he said. "Them, too."

And even though that was all he had to say about it, it was enough for me.

Just as we get to the truck, Grampa Peter puts his hand on my shoulder.

"Piel."

He has only said my name in Abenaki, but I understand. He's telling me that it's okay to watch the bus pull away. I can make it through this.

I turn around. I no longer hear the kid who is crying, and I hardly see the rest of the people gathered down there. All I see is the rear window of the bus and Mom looking out of it.

My eyesight is better than most. I can pick out things clearly at a distance when others just see a blur. Hawk eyes, Dad calls it, like a bird of prey seeing a mouse from way up in the sky. Mom has her hand raised, palm toward me. I raise mine back at her and I read her lips as she mouths three words: *I love you.*

I love you, too, Mom, I say silently, just before the bus takes a right turn onto Elm Street and she's gone.

Grampa Peter and I stand there. We probably look like two statues—one a tall, straight old man with a brown face and long white hair, and the other a gawky, long-limbed teenager.

Then Grampa moves his eyes upward, toward the peaks that tower over the town. I follow his gaze to the clouds that are starting to gather up there like flocks of sheep.

"Storm coming," he says.

Those words send a chill down my back.

CHAPTER THREE

Storm Coming

As soon as we get back, Grampa Peter and I shut the windows of the trailer, latch the door of the shed, cover up the young tomato plants, make sure the plastic over the woodpile is secure, and retie the tarps over our four-wheelers. It's a good thing we're moving fast. The wind hits the trailer just as I shut the last window.

Whap. It's as if a giant has swatted an immense hand against us. The thirty-foot trailer shudders like a nervous horse. Then the rain and hail hit hard against the aluminum roof and walls, creating a deafening roar.

I always like storms like this, but I like them even more when I'm outside. I've been coming to Grampa's trailer in New Hampshire for years and I've gotten to know all the best sheltering places on Mount Washington and Mount Jefferson, the mountains that rise above it. It's really amazing to be under a rock ledge or in the mouth of a cave in the heart of a storm.

Of course not everyone feels that way. To some it is just plain terrifying. Mount Washington, the tallest peak in the Northeast, is one of the most dangerous mountains in the world. Wind lives up there. That wind was once clocked at 233 miles per hour, the highest surface wind ever recorded. And Mount Washington is also often the coldest place in the lower forty-eight states. At its worst, figuring in wind chill, it can be just as cold on the summit as the deadliest winters in Antarctica. Every season hikers get lost up there; some die. Even the eight-mile-long road that winds 6,288 feet up the east side to the summit can be deadly. Cars get blown off of it in late summer, and it is closed to tourists in the winter.

You have to respect the mountain. It's not just a pile of rocks. It's alive, and there are times when it can really hurt you. The name Mount Washington makes it seem friendly, as familiar as the first president of the United States. People think of the mountain as being tamed. After all, there's an observatory on the top, ski runs on its slopes, and an old cog railway running along one side. There even used to be a hotel up there.

But my family remembers what our old people called it: Agiocochook. Some have translated that as "Home of the Great Spirit," and others have said it means the place where the storm wind blows. But neither is exactly right. The true meaning, "Where the Wind Spirit Is Alive," is far more ominous.

No one knows more about this part of our land than Grampa Peter. Sure, a geologist can speak about the formation of these mountains and valleys, a meteorologist can explain why the climate at the summit is so forbidding, and perhaps a historian could do a more scholarly job of talking about the European history of this place they now call New Hampshire that is still part of Ndakinna—Our Land—to us. But they don't know it from the heart and spirit the way he does.

What my Grampa knows is both as old as the wind and as present as the breath in our lungs. He knows how to talk to the mountains and has not forgotten how to listen to them. One big reason that he was such a popular wilderness guide before he retired was that no one ever got lost or hurt when he took them into the peaks. Hiking, rock climbing, cross-country skiing, canoeing. He did it all. He worked with scout groups and grown-ups and, believe it or not, he was a great storyteller.

"Scouts wear you out," he said once. Then he chuckled because he knew that I knew he was just joking. He really liked those kids, and they worshipped him. They thought he knew everything about the mountains. They weren't wrong.

I turn now to look out the window and I can no longer see anything other than a solid wash of water streaming down the glass. Behind me, Grampa Peter is getting the casserole ready to put into the oven. He's a good cook—as long as a meal involves bacon and anything that comes in a can. Baked beans are his specialty.

Good thing I like beans. I'll be eating them a lot until I learn to cook some of the recipes that Mom has left with me, all printed out neatly in green ink on color-coded five-by-seven-inch cards. Red cards are main dishes, yellow cards are sides, and white cards are desserts. Mom is nothing if not organized.

I pull out a white card at random. Tapioca. I open the left-hand cupboard, which has the foods arranged alphabetically starting with the bottles of applesauce way up top, and pull out a tapioca box from the lowest shelf.

I look at the picture on the box of the dessert, a yellowish-white mound, almost like the snow-covered peak of Agiocochook. A shiver runs down my spine. I close my eyes, and it's there. The dream I had last night is still with me.

I put down the dessert box and walk over to open the door. The storm has blown through as fast as it came, and a single hailstone, as big as the end of my thumb, is caught in the recessed aluminum strip across the outside screen door. I reach my hand around and grab it, holding it up to my forehead and then putting it into my mouth, letting it melt on my tongue.

It makes me feel calmer, this icy gift from the highest clouds where the Thunder Beings walk. It cools my insides. But my dream from last night haunts me. I am still running, still trying to hide from something I cannot see. I know that it sees me with eyes that can pierce the darkness. I know that it hungers to take my life.

CHAPTER FOUR

Dreams

I slump down in the old recliner in the living room of the trailer, remembering something my father once told me: "If a dream is troubling you, find a quiet place to sit down, close your eyes, and run through it in your mind."

Sometimes it doesn't work, but when I close my eyes now, it's as if I am right back in the dream. I can't see the monster, but I can sense it. It's above me, swooping down on wide, leathery wings, its arms spread out to grab me with talons glistening in the light from the full moon.

I open my eyes and it's gone. I take a deep breath.

In my family, we believe that dreams can be more than just your subconscious acting out its insecurities. Sometimes they are warnings. And when it is something as clear as the winged creature in my dream, it's a warning you need to take seriously.

I stand up and go to the window. I can see the peak of Mount Washington in the distance. Few of our people ever climbed it before the Europeans came here to our land. The first white man to make his way to the top did so more than 350 years ago, in 1642. He was a Puritan named Darby Field. One story is that he thought he would find riches up there. But all he found was a bare, rocky peak, and he came down in disappointment. Our old people said he was lucky to come down at all.

Some people wonder why Field thought there was something precious hidden on top of the mountain. I don't. Because even though all that greedy man found was the wind and the stones, our old stories tell of something more that remains up there to this day.

Pmola.

And Pmola's treasure.

My mom first told me about Pmola's treasure when I was in fourth grade. The teacher had sent each of us home with an assignment to collect a story from someone in our family.

Mom and Dad had looked at each other, one of those looks that told me they were both thinking the exact same thing. Then Mom had nodded her head. "Tell Paul the story about Pmola's ring," she said to Dad. "It belongs to you Fortunes."

So Dad did.

Long ago, an Abenaki hunter was following the trail of a wounded deer high up the slopes of Wanbi Wadzoak, the big white mountains. When he looked back across the valley, he saw that a storm was blowing in and he quickly crawled into a narrow cave in the mountainside. The storm lasted a long time, and the hunter fell asleep. Night had fallen by the time he woke up. When he looked outside, the moon's reflection was glistening on the face of a pond known as Small Lake of the Clouds.

The hunter had gone past Small Lake of the Clouds when he took shelter. Now, after having slept, he felt thirsty and thought of going out to drink from that pond. But an uneasy feeling held him back. He realized that when he had passed the water on his way to seek shelter, he had not seen the dark boulder that was now by the edge of the pond. The hunter froze then, for it seemed as if that dark boulder was moving. As he watched, dark wings unfolded from it and the crouched figure stood up.

The hunter held his breath. He recognized the winged being as Pmola, the powerful creature that was said to have its lair atop the high peak. Almost no one ventured up there, and if they were foolish or brave enough to try, they never returned alive.

Pmola turned and looked in the hunter's direction. The hunter closed his eyes. When he opened them again, he saw that Pmola was no longer looking his way, but bending to turn over a big stone. As the hunter watched in fascination, Pmola placed something glittering under that stone before rolling it back in place. Then the wide wings spread, flapped once, and Pmola lifted up into the air and disappeared into the night.

The hunter waited, uncertain of what to do. He shuddered at the thought of what might happen if he came out too soon and Pmola saw him. But then an idea came to him. It was said that every powerful creature had a source of strength that it kept hidden. If anyone found that source, the creature would be at their mercy, too weak to harm them. Perhaps, the hunter thought, that glittering object held

Pmola's strength. If he could gain control of it, it might protect him from the monster.

The hunter looked up to the sky, where the Night Traveler, the grandmother moon, was showing half of her face. "Grandmother," the hunter whispered, "protect me." Then he slipped out of the cave and made his way down to the Small Lake of the Clouds and the stone by which Pmola had crouched. His hands found something hard and smooth. He pulled it out and held it up, watching it glisten silver in the moonlight. Then, the hair on the back of his neck stood up. The hunter turned to see Pmola looming over him, clawed hands reaching out.

Still clutching the glittering thing he had pulled from its hiding place under the stone, the frightened man took a step backward and then another as Pmola slowly came toward him. Soon the hunter found himself at the edge of a cliff with a long drop to the rocks below. There was nowhere further to retreat. Pmola spread its leathery wings wide and opened its mouth, showing teeth sharper and longer than those of any wolf.

Then Pmola screamed.

CHAPTER FIVE

Captain Hook

That was where Dad ended that story the first time he told it. Talk about a cliffhanger! And that's where I'll end it right now because I can hear someone knocking on the door of our trailer. I am sure that Grampa Peter also hears it, even though he's out back by the woodpile. Old as he is, his ears are better than anyone else's I've ever known—which is saying something since everyone in our family has really good hearing. We joke that our hearing is so good that when we go fishing, we can hear the fish dappling the surface on the other side of the lake. But Grampa Peter's hearing is so good that he can hear the fish swimming underwater!

Ever since I was a tiny kid, he's used little sound signals to send me messages. There's this certain call he uses, a little like a chickadee's but longer, to let me know when he's around before I've seen him. If he thumps the ground twice with his foot, like a rabbit does to warn its little ones, I know that danger is near and I should stay still and not move. And a long whistle, like that of a red-tailed hawk, means to come quickly because he needs help.

Now, though, he's not making any sounds aside from the noise of one piece of wood being placed on top of another as he rearranges the pile—which seemed perfectly fine before he started working on it.

I guess this means that he wants whoever is knocking to go away. Or maybe he wants me to be the one to open the door? Probably choice numero uno. But curiosity has always gotten the better of me—or the worse in some cases—so I go to the door, open it, and look down to see who is standing on our steps.

Then I look up. The guy who was doing the knocking is actually almost even with me, despite my height and the fact that the trailer door is two feet above the bottom step, where he's standing.

But while he's tall enough to be a center in the NBA, his face isn't like that of a basketball player. It sort of resembles one of the bad guys in those *Pirates of the Caribbean* films or maybe the cartoon Captain Hook. He has dark eyebrows, a pointy, oiled mustache, long black hair that falls to his shoulders, and a grin on his face that looks more painted-on than friendly. But what makes him even stranger is what he's wearing. Not a buccaneer getup like his appearance from the neck up might lead you to expect. Instead, he's got on a three-piece suit that probably cost as much as our trailer—when it was new. The trailer, I mean, not the suit. And by the way I'm talking now you can tell how confused I'm feeling.

But I don't let it show. I keep my face expressionless—unlike those eyes of his, which glitter with some kind of recognition as he studies my face. Like I am the answer to some problem that's been bothering him. Or maybe, on second thought, like a hungry man looking at a Big Mac.

"Ah," he says, in a voice peculiarly high for someone so big, "you must be the grandson."

I don't say anything. How do you respond to something like that?

His smile broadens. This time it's a look straight out of that same Peter Pan cartoon. Not from Captain Hook, though. The crocodile.

"Not so?" he asks. He's got a strong English accent. I still don't answer him. "It must be that you are his relative," he continues. "A grandson, no? You are most assuredly as taciturn as the old man. So where is he?"

The answer to that is right behind him, where Grampa Peter has come up so quietly and suddenly that even I didn't see his approach.

"Here," Grampa Peter says in a voice that is both quiet and strong.

Captain Hook spins halfway around and almost trips over his own feet. He doesn't fall, but he's unhappy about being taken by surprise and the phony smile is momentarily wiped off his face, replaced by a look that combines impatience, displeasure . . . and menace. If I felt leery about this guy before, I for sure don't like or trust him now.

He recovers himself quickly, though. The expression of insincere friendliness pops back onto his face as quick as a rattlesnake striking.

"Mr. Fortune," Captain Hook pipes, "so nice to see you again." He holds out a hand toward Grampa Peter—who does something

I have never seen him do before. Instead of taking the man's hand in that ancient gesture of truce between enemies or trust between friends, Grampa Peter folds his arms and raises one eyebrow.

"Nope," he says, keeping his gaze on the ground.

Wow! This guy really is bad news!

Captain Hook turns to me. "Talk some sense into your grandfather," he hisses. "We'll make it worth his while if he assists us."

He turns back toward the extended-cab Chevy that is parked at the end of our walkway with the passenger door left open. There's a woman behind the wheel wearing big hoop earrings. I can't make out her features because she has on a Yankees cap that shades her face, but I can see that her brown hair, woven into a braid that falls over her shoulder, is even longer than Captain Hook's.

As he reaches the truck, Captain Hook, who I now realize is wearing built-up boots with heels that have increased his height by at least five inches, turns back to glare at us both.

"And if you foolishly choose not to help us," he snarls, "you shall indeed regret it."

He throws himself into the cab and slams the

door. The truck peels out, throwing an arc of gravel from its fishtailing rear wheels.

Grampa Peter can tell how confused I am by the look on my face. He gestures for me to go inside and sit down on our mini couch, which I do, knees up around my ears as usual. He follows me and starts sorting through the remotes to find the ones that control, respectively, the high-def flat-screen TV and one of his Sony DVD players.

Grampa Peter may be an old guy in his sixties who knows more about the traditional ways than almost anyone I know, but he loves modern gadgets. The whole western wall of the trailer is taken up by an assemblage of turntables, stereos, tape players, TVs of various shapes and sizes, computer monitors, Super 8s, VCRs, DVD units, even a Blu-ray player that showed up three days ago. Everything works, too. Plus the shelves under the equipment are chock-full of records and tapes, discs and DVDs, all arranged according to a system I don't understand, but one that makes it possible for Grampa Peter to put his hands on anything he wants in a matter of seconds. It might be an old episode of *Rawhide* (Grampa Peter loves Clint Eastwood) or a documentary on the Yanomami people of the Amazon.

Or maybe something about his two favorite people from the twentieth century—Harry Houdini, the escape artist, and a comedian named Lenny Bruce, both of whom he says could have been Indians.

An unmarked DVD seems to fall of its own accord off the top of a pile right into his left hand. He slips it into the Sony, slides in next to me on the couch, and presses a few buttons. A convoluted eight-armed figure that looks vaguely Tibetan fills the twenty-four-inch flat screen.

FORBIDDEN MYSTERIES read the words in red twisty letters at the bottom.

Grampa Peter turns up the volume as a face fills the screen. A high, insistent voice with an English accent rises in midsentence.

". . . truth of the Mothman Prophecy will be revealed. Such beings as these that have haunted our dreams, do they truly exist? And are they here among us now? What secrets or treasures do they guard? Come with me, your intrepid host, Darby Field the fourth, as we seek the truth of another Forbidden Mystery!"

I feel a chill go down my back. What was that name he called himself? Did I hear it right?

The figure is replaced by a rough drawing of a birdlike creature with no head and two

31

red eyes staring out of its chest. It morphs into another image. This one is not a drawing, but a photograph of what archaeologists call an "artifact" and my people call a sacred object. A second chill goes down my back.

I've seen it before. It was on display in the Fruitlands Museum in Harvard, Massachusetts. It was made of sheet copper, probably fashioned from a kettle obtained through trade with white people back in the seventeenth century, and stood about ten inches tall. Its body shape was sort of like that of the figure in the drawing and there were two holes in the chest area about where the eyes were here. The label on the case said that it had been "recovered" from Amoskeag Falls in Manchester, New Hampshire. Not that far from here.

The museum people described it as a "thunderbird." I didn't try to correct anyone about what it really was or tell them they really ought to return it to the place it came from. I also didn't tell them who it really depicted. Pmola. I just whispered to the sacred object in Abenaki and let it know I sympathized with it having to be locked in a case and that I hoped it wouldn't feel so bad that it would bring harm to anyone.

Grampa Peter pushes the pause button on the remote and turns to me. He knows I've seen enough.

"Hmm?" he says.

My heart is beating like I've just run a hundred-yard dash.

"Did I hear that guy's name right?" I ask.

"Uh-huh." Grampa Peter nods.

I take a deep breath to calm myself. I'd recognized the voice and face of Darby Field IV, the host of *Forbidden Mysteries*. How could I not, with that superior, sneering tone, those leering eyes, that black mustache, long hair, and toothy grin? Captain Hook.

CHAPTER SIX

Pmola's Treasure

I need to know what this Darby Field wants from us. I can tell by the look on Grampa Peter's face that he is thinking about how best to explain things, so I don't ask anything as we walk out back to where he has his smudge fire going to keep away mosquitoes and the other little biting creatures that want our blood. He sits on a tree stump on one side of the fire, and I sit down across from him. He drops a small green cedar bough onto the fire and watches the smoke curl up.

"First of all," Grampa says, "don't believe anything he says. Not even who he claims t' be. Uses that phony accent to impress people. He's English, I'm an Irish potato."

Grampa Peter chuckles at his own joke.

34

"Who is he, then?" I ask. Grampa's joke has calmed me a little. But the name Darby Field means something to us. This has to be more than just coincidence.

"Heard his real name's Schmidt. Maybe he just took on *Darby Field* because it sounded good." Grampa Peter pokes at the fire with a stick. A few sparks rise up. "Maybe, though, that name chose him. He's got the same kind of arrogant greed that first Darby Field had. Only thing you can trust about him is that he's out to get whatever he can."

Grampa Peter reaches out to pull his hand back through the smoke, bringing some of it up so that it washes over his white hair. Then he waves his hand to waft some in my direction, and I cup both my palms to bring the smoke back to me. Cedar smoke is cleansing, drives away bad influences.

"First time he came here was a week ago. Said he'd heard how much I knew about the old ways. Wanted me to tell him about the mysteries of the mountain for one of his TV specials. Show him things."

Grampa Peter swings his hand off to the side, palm up, as if he's throwing something away. It's one of our old sign language gestures: *No way is that going to happen.* He looks over at me to see if I understand.

I nod.

"But that's not what he really wants," Grampa Peter says.

"Pmola's treasure," I say.

"Yup."

Great, I think. Too many things happening all at once. My thoughts go back to my dream of trying to escape from winged death. Those who are *medawlinno,* like some in my family, often have dreams that come true. And messing with Pmola is the last thing anyone in my family would ever want to do.

Not that Pmola is evil. I think back to that story my dad told me, the one he finally finished two nights after he'd started it. My imagination had done a good job of filling in the blanks, and I had woken up two nights in a row from dreams in which black wings wrapped around me, sharp claws dug into my shoulders, and long fangs sought my throat.

But what really happened, Dad said, was this:

When Pmola screamed, the man didn't do what some people might have done. That man was a hunter and he had observed how predators like the owl and the mountain lion scream to make their prey freeze so that it is easier to grab them. So the hunter didn't just stand there. He dove to the side and scrambled into a narrow crevice in the rocks. Pmola's claws scratched the hunter's ankle, but the winged monster was too large to follow him into that place of refuge.

Then Pmola spoke. Its voice was a blend of the whistling storm wind and an eagle's cry.

"Mmmmy ring," Pmola shrilled. "Give mmme mmmy ring. Give it to mmme and I will give yooouuu a gift."

The hunter realized he was still holding that object he'd found hidden under the stone by Small Lake of the Clouds. He held it up to look at it. It was a large golden ring. Even in the darkness of the crevice, it glittered as if it were on fire. It was beautiful, but the man valued his life more than a ring of gold.

"Pmola," the man said, "I do not want to steal your power. I only took this ring to protect myself. All I ask is that you let me go free if I return it to you," the man said.

Pmola thrust its hand into the crevice. "Mmmmy ring," it cried again, "Give mmme mmmy ring."

The man dropped the ring into the palm of Pmola's long, clawed hand. As soon as he did so, that hand was snatched back and the hunter heard the sound of wings beating the air. Then all was silent.

The man waited a long time before coming out of that crevice. He looked cautiously in all directions, but Pmola was gone. From then on, even though he had asked for no gift other than his own life, that hunter had great good luck. But he never again went anywhere near Small Lake of the Clouds.

Pmola, you see, despises dishonesty and greed. If that man in the story hadn't given Pmola back his ring or had tried to trick Pmola, you can bet that something bad would have happened to him. Something really bad. Which is why he didn't ask for anything special. Not wealth or power. Just his life. And because he was not greedy, he was given more than he asked for.

I'd be happy if the lives of my own family were safe. If Mom and Dad were not over there and if Grampa Peter and I didn't have someone trying to pull us into something ominous here. Was my dream about Pmola a warning or a foretelling?

"So what do we do?" I ask Grampa Peter.

And I immediately feel dumb because I know what his answer will be.

But he smiles at me as he says it.

"Nothing."

CHAPTER SEVEN

Stuck

Nothing. That is sometimes the strongest answer you can give to someone who asks you a dumb question.

But even so, as I lie in bed and listen to the wind outside our trailer, I am thinking that saying nothing, and doing nothing, is not going to satisfy Captain Hook or Darby Field or Schmidt or whoever he really is. I saw the angry look on his face and the greed in his eyes.

Our old stories tell us to be wary of that kind of anger and greed. It can twist a person inside out, and dry up all the good they might have once had in them. As Grampa Peter says, it's not that there are good guys and bad guys, white hats and black hats. Everybody has the potential for doing good and doing bad. However, when people give themselves over to their worst impulses—greed, jealousy, anger, revenge—they can sometimes crawl so far over the edge, and down into those twisted thoughts, that they're never able to find their way back up.

I know in my heart that I've looked into the eyes of one of those who left his better self behind so long ago that doing good isn't even a distant memory. Whoever he is, Darby Field, and everything about him, is bad news.

And I can't get to sleep. It's not just because I can't stop thinking about this threatening man. And it's not just that whenever I'm not thinking about that, I find myself worrying about Mom and Dad.

No, I've actually managed to turn off those worried thoughts—almost long enough to go to sleep. I've learned how to do this routine where I concentrate first on relaxing my toes, just my toes. Then I relax my calves, then my knees, and so on up the long length of my body until by the time I reach my head—or sometimes even before that—I've fallen asleep.

Problem is, every time I relax my legs, they cramp up because this bed is too short. I can't straighten out the way I usually do when I've managed to get my whole body to go limp.

I'm almost there, and then my heels fall off the bottom of the bed and my toes stick out from under the covers, and I am wide awake again.

Dang it!

I sit up, swing my legs out, and slip my feet into my old soft-soled mocs. I strip the sheets and blankets off the bed and then, in one of those habits you pick up in a military family, I fold them neatly and place them on the chair. I know it sounds anal-retentive, but I just don't feel comfortable in a messy room. I take the mattress off the bed and lean it against the wall to study the bed frame. I look back and forth and then nod. My idea ought to work.

I open the drawer of the bedside table where I've placed one of my favorite things from my dad. It's a little Maglite attached to a Velcro headband. It leaves your hands free and you can just turn your head to point the beam wherever you want to light up the darkness. I wrap the headband around my forehead so that the light is on the side just above my right eye and then I press the switch. The high-intensity beam makes a circle the size of a basketball on my bed.

I turn off the light as I tiptoe out into the hall. I don't want to bother Grampa Peter and

I know I can find my way around in the dark. I don't trip over any of the chairs or tables, even though there's not a lot of space between things in the cramped hallway and the tiny living room. I have a great memory. Once I've been somewhere, I can picture it perfectly in my mind. But I am going to need light when I'm outside.

I open the door, slip out, and close it slowly behind me so that it doesn't bang. No problem. When I'm by myself, I'm hardly ever clumsy. It's just when I'm in front of people. However, now I turn the light on. Sure, I remember everything that I might bump into or trip over on my way to the back of our trailer, where Grampa Peter has things stored. But on a summer night like this there might be some other things out in the darkness that were not there when the sun went down. Furry things drawn by the smell of our garbage pails that are locked securely in the little shed. Raccoons are not so bad because they'll back away as soon as a human comes close. Skunks, though, are either too confident or stupid to leave, and I do not want to upset a skunk! There is also the chance that a bear might be out there. Again, nothing to worry about if you give the bear fair warning, but bears do not take kindly to being surprised. Not that a bear will usually try to attack, but if a bear feels cornered and you are between it and its preferred escape route, well, too bad for you.

I sweep the light from side to side as I walk slowly around the trailer and out back. No midnight garbage snackers. Not even a mouse. Probably discouraged by this noisy wind, which is bending the birch trees up and down like someone trying to string a bow and then changing his mind.

I get down on my knees and elbows and lift my chin to direct the beam under the trailer. Grampa Peter has all his spare building and repair supplies stored in precise stacks in the twenty-eight-inch-high space between the concrete slab and the floor. Cinder blocks to the left. Patio blocks next to them. Bags of sand and mortar mix up on pallets and covered with plastic. Lumber to the far left. A pile of two-by-fours, another of pressure-treated planks, and a third pile of miscellaneous lumber. There, right on top of the third, is just what I remembered: a six-foot-long by four-foot-wide piece of three-quarter-inch plywood. I can make my bed longer by putting this piece under my mattress so that it sticks out at the bottom. Then if I put two couch pillows between the wall and the top end, I will have solved my sleeping problems.

I can't help smiling, the circle of light bobbing up and down as I nod my head. I'm a genius.

I bend low and crawl in. An orb weaver spider has made her web across the upper left-hand corner of the opening. Grampa Peter pointed her out to me with a nod of his head when I arrived here. He didn't have to tell me to respect her. We don't have some of those stories that the Indians in the Southeast and the West have about the spider being a grandmother, but we know that spiders catch those little insects that like to bite us, so we show them respect.

There's plenty of room for me to get under the trailer without disturbing her intricate weaving, and I'm sure I'll be able to shove the plywood out underneath the web when I work it free.

But it may take some doing. That three-quarter-inch piece of plywood is heavier than I thought. I grab it with one hand and pull. It doesn't budge. I try taking hold of it with both hands. I don't have any leverage at all and once again the plywood stays put. But I don't. I lose my balance and fall forward, scraping my hand against the rough edge of the plywood sheet.

Double dang! I hold my right hand up to

my mouth so I can use my teeth to pull out the splinter I've just stuck an inch deep into my palm.

As I suck on the wound, I try to think. What is it that Mom always says? If you can't make things work one way, try doing the opposite? Yes! I roll over onto my back, hook my feet under the edge of the trailer, and reach back over my head to pull the plywood toward me. One, two, hup! Success! The plywood comes free from whatever was holding it, slides smoothly forward, and then stops. Right on top of me!

I'm sort of stuck. Also the plywood has hit the switch on my Maglite, and I am now in total darkness. I pull my legs in so I can wiggle onto my side and get out from under the wide piece of pressed lumber that is making me feel like the cheese in a sandwich.

I try to do it as quietly as possible, without knocking against any of the supports under the trailer floor. The wind has suddenly died down and the night is quiet.

Or is it? Are those boots crunching the gravel of our walkway? I hear the thud of feet hitting the trailer steps at a run and the sound of the front door—right over my head—bursting open as a heavy body hurls itself against it!

CHAPTER EIGHT

Got Him

"The old man first!" A thin reedy voice with an English accent.

"Got him." The second male voice is one that I haven't heard before. Unlike Darby Field, this man has a nasal South Boston accent.

"Where's the kid?" A woman's voice with the kind of hoarseness in it that comes from smoking too many cigarettes.

Three of them. I start trying to struggle out from under the board that has me trapped. I don't know what I'm going to do, but I have to do something. Run for help, try to fight them.

Suddenly two loud thumps come from right over my head. Spaced just right so there is no doubt what they mean. Grampa Peter must have been awake and aware of what I was doing all the while I was creeping around and crawling under the house. Those stomps on the floor are his signal to me.

Stay where you are!

I freeze in place, but I keep listening.

"Where's your grandson?"

No answer, of course.

"I know how to make him talk," South Boston growls.

There's the sound of a scuffle, a thud, a groan, a body falling to the floor.

"Unh, unh, unh . . . you old . . . unh, unh."

It's not Grampa Peter who's rolling on the floor in pain, but South Boston. The man obviously never learned that it isn't wise to try to muscle a Marine—even one who's in his late sixties.

The woman with the hoarse voice is laughing. "Come on, Tippy. Get up. This can't be the first time you got kicked in the groin."

There's the sound of furniture being pushed aside, a man pulling himself to his feet.

I tense up, afraid of what he's going to do now to Grampa Peter.

"I'm gonna break your—," the man called Tippy begins to growl.

But Darby Field's voice cuts in. "Tip, you can forget about physical persuasion. Now back off like a good lad. And you, sir, if you try anything like that again, I shall put a twenty-two-caliber slug into your knee. Sit down. Excellent. Now Louise is going to do a bit of scouting around to see if she can locate your beanpole of a grandson."

Feet walking across the floor, the door opening and closing, the wide beam of a heavy-duty flashlight visible through the cracks in the apron that goes around the base of the trailer.

I slowly pull my knees up to my chest. I hope I can't be seen under here. I put my hand over the luminous dial of my watch. I don't want to risk the chance that its glow will give me away. I also look down at the ground. Eyes reflect back the beam of a light. Also there's this sort of sixth sense that all people have, the feeling you get when someone is looking at you. If you don't believe me, try staring hard at someone's back and see if they don't turn around. Or try looking at the face of the driver of a car coming at you in the opposite lane. Nine times out of ten that driver will make eye contact back.

Louise—she must have been the woman with the Yankees cap and long brown braid

in Field's truck—is making her way around the trailer slowly, methodically. The way she's moving, though, gives me hope. Her steps are tentative. She's bumping against things, almost falling, and catching herself. She's obviously one of those city people who is not used to such dark. The strong scent of her perfume, which I could smell even through the floor of the trailer, is getting closer. I sense her crouching at the opening under the trailer.

"Huuuh," she mutters to herself as her beam of light reflects off the web of my orb weaver friend, "spiders." The light is directed away, and her feet move off.

"Thank you," I mouth to the spider, who has just repaid my respect by protecting me.

CHAPTER NINE

Looking

"No sign of the boy," Louise says. She's back in the house with the others.

"And a great help you were," Field says in a sarcastic voice.

"Hey, I'm a soundperson, not bleedin' Chingachgook or Pocahontas. You want an Indian guide, don't look at me."

"My dear," Field replies, with the long-suffering tone of a genius having to deal with idiots, "that is precisely why we are obtaining the services of our elderly and stubborn friend Mr. Fortune here." He chuckles. "To guide us to fame and fortune. But that grandson of his was to be our means of, one might say, gentle persuasion."

"From the looks of his room," Tip says, "He wasn't here tonight. His bed ain't even made."

"Maybe he's sleeping over at a friend's house," Louise suggests.

"Hmmmph," Field says. "Just finish duct-taping the old man's hands together—at the wrists and the elbows, Louise. From what I've seen, Mr. Fortune here may not be an easy one to control. No, leave his legs free. He has a bit of walking to do. And Tip, do keep him out of the frame when we're shooting. No visual evidence. Just the trail, scenery, and then close on me."

The door opens and the steps creak as a heavy person puts his weight on them, takes a deep breath.

"Oh, Pauuuul!"

I almost jump at the sound of my name. The "come-out, come-out, wherever you are" tone to Darby Field's voice tells me he's just calling into the night on the chance I might be within earshot.

"We have your grandfaaather."

Smug, self-assured. If I were standing out in the darkness beyond the trailer and I had a rock, I'd heave it at him. But I stay put.

"What's the matter, lad? We shan't hurt you" —then—under his breath—"much." He clears his throat. "But we will certainly begin doing some rather severe physical harm to your grandfather if you don't assist us."

The thought of what they might do to Grampa Peter if I don't do what he asks almost makes me decide to give myself up. But I'm not stupid. I remember what Dad and Mom told me about hostage takers, how the only thing that makes them happier than having one hostage is having two.

And I think of other lessons they taught me:

Don't ever give up an advantage in combat.

Don't let your emotions get the better of you.

Think one or two steps ahead of your enemy.

I don't know much about Darby Field, but I know I can't trust him. He wants to use me to make Grampa Peter lead him to Pmola's treasure.

That familiar chill runs down my back. It's bad enough to have a greedy person threatening your life. But Darby Field isn't just greedy. He wants to find a creature that most people think is just a myth, and the legendary treasure that belongs to that creature. That is just plain crazy.

I remember one of the stories Grampa Peter told me about a day when he was out in a canoe with an Abenaki friend of his. It was getting close to dusk when they saw something in the sky.

"Look," his friend said. "It is the Old One with Wings. I will call him down."

"Don't," Grampa Peter said.

But his friend didn't listen. He made a gesture and spoke some words. Pretty soon that winged thing up in the sky began to circle down closer. It was bigger than a hawk. Bigger than an eagle.

Grampa Peter's friend began to get worried. "I will send him back," he said.

But his voice was uncertain as he raised his hand to make another gesture and spoke. And that big winged shape just kept getting closer. Now they could see its red eyes.

"Help me," his friend pleaded.

"Here!" Grampa Peter replied, digging in his paddle to turn their canoe toward the shore.

As soon as they hit the beach, Grampa Peter jumped out and ran toward a huge old pine that had been tipped over by a high wind, his friend close behind him. There was a hole in the blue clay bank at the base of the tree, made by the roots pulling out of the ground. Grampa Peter dove into that hole, turned, and pulled his friend in after him. A hard wind was blowing by then, and other trees were starting to fall.

The two of them huddled together until the wind stopped.

When they came out and went back down to the shore, they saw that they had a long walk ahead of them. Their canoe had been torn to pieces, their paddles broken into bits.

"Look for trouble," Grampa Peter said, "trouble finds you."

Does Darby Field have any idea of the kind of things that can still happen? Or does he think that all those mysteries he's chasing are harmless? Our stories about monsters remind us that only a fool goes in search of one of our old powerful beings.

I shake my head. He won't hurt Grampa Peter while he's trying to find me to use as leverage. If I want to help my grandfather, I have to avoid being caught, no matter what.

And there is another thing that I know for sure. This man's plans—if he intends to continue being the star of his own TV show—don't include leaving witnesses around when he commits crimes like he's just committed. Home invasion, assault, kidnapping.

Once he gets what he wants, he's going to kill us.

CHAPTER TEN

Stay Put

I'm still under the trailer and they're still in the living room. All three of them. Not Grampa Peter, though. He was put into the little storage room right next to the bathroom.

"For safekeeping," Field said as he shoved my grandfather in there. I heard Grampa Peter sit down hard as if he lost his balance, banging his hands twice on the floor.

Stay put.

And now Field's gang is sitting upstairs in the dark, in case I come home and walk in without realizing they are there. From what they said to each other, they have hidden the truck down the road where there's a pull-off among the birch trees.

It's been surprisingly easy to listen in on what they've said and to tell what is going on from the sounds above. I never realized before just how thin the floor of the trailer is. Where there's no rug to muffle the sound, every noise comes through as clearly as if I were in the next room.

I hear them moving around, going back and forth to the kitchen area, getting coffee, looking into our refrigerator, just generally making themselves at home. But they're not watching TV or listening to music, and they're keeping their voices down. Definitely waiting for me to come back.

I look at my watch. 4:30 A.M. There're still two more hours until first light. One of them walks overhead, opens and closes a door. A few minutes later the toilet flushes and water goes gurgling through the pipes six feet from me. I find myself thinking of some of the adventure stories I've read in which a hero is in a tight place. But none of those heroes ever seem to have to go to the bathroom! I can't stay here forever!

I try to think logically. It's late and they won't be nearly as alert now as they were four hours ago when they burst in. And I have to get out of here.

57

I have been tensing and untensing my arms and legs to keep from getting cramps, so it's not that difficult for me to start moving. I lift the piece of plywood and begin sliding it back, a finger's width at a time. It makes a very soft shushing sound, but I'm sure that I'm the only one who hears it. When the plywood is no longer bearing down on me, I start to move myself. I do it just a little at a time, bending around so that when I come out from under the trailer I do so headfirst. I pause to look around and listen. They're still up there. No one has heard me.

It's dark, but the half-moon that is low in the sky to the west is casting enough light for me to start moving. I stay below the window, hugging the side of the trailer until I reach the edge that I know isn't visible from inside. I keep low and move like a stalking panther toward the trees and brush that are fifty feet beyond the backyard. There's still a wood-smoke smell rising from the fire pit, and the scent of burnt cedar gives me courage. I have a plan now. It's not much of one, but it might work.

There's a little trail in the brush and trees. Most people wouldn't be able to spot it, but I find it easily and begin to move more swiftly. I'm not completely silent, but the small noises of an occasional twig crunching under my feet or a branch brushing my shirt are sounds that blend in with the night. As soon as I'm far enough away, I relieve myself. Then I start climbing the hill. From what Field said, their truck should be parked on the other side where the road bends back. Just before I reach the hilltop, I stop again and place both my hands against my favorite big birch tree.

Its smooth bark is reassuring to me. We have a special relationship with the birch, which always gave us its bark in the old days to cover our lodges or to make baskets. We call it the blanket tree. By the moonlight I can see the black marks on the white trunk, marks that look like birds with widespread wings. Those are the marks of the eagle whose eyes shoot lightning. Elders say that if you stand under a birch tree when there's a thunderstorm, you'll never be hit by a lightning bolt.

I take a deep breath. "Am I doing the right thing?" I whisper to the tree.

Of course it gives me the same reply Grampa Peter would: a silence that reminds me to look into my own heart for the answer.

Go for it.

CHAPTER ELEVEN

No Sounds

I'm at the top of the hill now, looking down toward the road. The moonlight is glinting off something metallic in the pull-off under the birch trees. That has to be it.

I make my way down the path, stopping every three or four steps to look and listen. Nothing. No sounds, no sign of anything or anyone moving.

I'm closer now and I can see that it's the same truck that peeled away from our trailer.

I sit down while I'm still fifty feet away to run through my options. If the truck is unlocked and the key is inside, I'll climb in, start it up, and drive the three miles to town for help. I don't have a driver's license, but I know what I'm doing. I learned how to ride a mini motorbike when I was four. Then, when I was ten, and tall enough to reach the pedals, Dad put me behind the wheel of a Jeep. It was only on wood trails and off-road in fields, but it was real driving nonetheless. Dad would sit next to me with his hands behind his head saying, "Show me what you can do, Tiger."

If the door is unlocked but there is no key, I should still be able to take it. Mechanics is one of Mom's specialties—Humvees, half-tracks, tanks, it doesn't matter. Mom can take apart and put together any and all of them. So while Dad taught me how to drive everything from a dirt bike to an extended-cab truck, Mom gave me the lowdown on the workings of the internal combustion engine and every possible package you might put around it. That included certain things that almost no one my age would ever be taught by their parents—like how to hot-wire a car.

Yes, we are truly an unconventional family. Now it's time for me to repay the trust my parents put in me by taking charge and rescuing my grandfather.

I feel inside my pocket for my miniature Maglite and my Leatherman utility tool. The

Leatherman prepares me for my third option—if I can't get into the truck or I can't get it started, I'll use the fold-out lock knife to flatten all four tires. Then I'll head for town on foot.

Should work. But I'm hesitant to get up. There's no sight or sound of anything threatening, but I have a vague feeling of disquiet. Something is not right, but I can't figure out what it is.

I'm trying to be calm the way Grampa Peter always is, the way Mom and Dad tell me you have to be when you are in a combat zone. I've heard stories about people who lost their cool in a firefight and emptied their guns in the air or ran around in circles when the enemy was about to overrun the perimeter. If not for one or two clear heads taking charge, staying calm and knowing what to do, all would have been lost.

I take a deep breath. I look at my watch. 5:15 A.M. It may feel as if I have been sitting here for hours, but it's been only forty-five minutes since I climbed out from under the trailer. From my perch up here I can see the road and there's been no one on it. There's no other way any of them could have gotten back to the truck without taking the shortcut I took through the woods. And from what I have seen of that crew, none of them

62

are terribly comfortable in the forest. They would have stuck to the paved road for sure.

It's now or never. I get up and make my way to the truck. Still quiet all around. I reach for the door handle. As I pull it, I hear the click of the latch opening.

And just like that, with that sound, it comes to me. As I open the door and the light inside the cab comes on, I realize what is wrong: the silence.

No sounds of crickets or little animals stirring in the brush, no call of an owl from the woods. The kind of quiet you have when something big is lurking nearby.

I'm an idiot! I let go of the door handle and turn to run, but it's too late. Something grabs me from behind and lifts me up into the air.

CHAPTER TWELVE

The Catch

Well, I got my wish. I'm in the truck, though not at all in the way I imagined it. I'm propped up in the passenger seat with my hands and feet secured by duct tape and another strip firmly over my mouth. A very large man with shoulders like a gorilla is sitting behind the wheel. He was businesslike in his efficiency as he wrapped me up. Rough, but not brutal about it when he saw that I wasn't going to fight. When he turned me around and I looked up into his face, I saw that resistance would be futile. Plus—and this is another lesson learned from a military family—when you are in a situation where overcoming your enemy isn't possible, don't waste your strength. Don't give up hope, but wait. Sooner or later, there may be a chance to escape.

"Hold out hands."

His accent was like Arnold Schwarzenegger's and his face was covered in scars and set in a big square head topped by a shaved dome. It was what Mom jokingly calls a Dieter face. Like a map of Germany. There was no anger in this Dieter's expression, but also no more pity than a cat would show to a mouse it just caught.

I held out my hands and he pinned my wrists together with one paw that was at least as broad as that of a bear. He treated taking a hostage like it was an everyday thing, which I suspect it was before he joined Darby Field.

I look over at him now, trying to see what else I can figure out about him from the way he looks. Not much beyond his obvious military past. I suspect that what you see is what you get with Dieter—or Otto or Bruno or whatever this guy's name is. Former East German army maybe. A mercenary soldier now, for sure. I should have figured that Field would have at least one person in his entourage who was an experienced head basher.

The funny thing is, now that I am a captive myself, I no longer feel frantic. Like my dad used to say, you never know how you're going to react to combat until you have your first real encounter with the enemy. Some people just can't handle it. But others, even though they're nervous before it happens, are fine once the firing starts. They find the calm in the eye of the storm.

I almost smile.

Yes, I know that's weird, seeing as how I have failed in my first mission and I am about to be put in the one role I didn't want to play. If this were a movie, I'd be the stock figure who gets held captive and threatened with death or torture by the bad guys in order to make the hero do their bidding.

"Open the safe or we'll cut off another one of his fingers."

"Give us the secret code or we'll break his other leg."

"Show us where you've hidden the map or we'll push him into the snake pit."

But none of that scares me now. Part of it is that I was never afraid of getting hurt myself. I was afraid of what would happen to Grampa Peter.

Now that the weight of being the sole hope for my grandfather is gone, I'm finally thinking one step ahead. I'm seeing things not just through my own eyes but through those of Grampa Peter. It's as if I can hear his voice in my head. And maybe I can.

I think of how Dad once explained to me why Grampa Peter was always so quiet. "He believes what our old people believed. Not saying much out loud makes talking without words stronger. You have to listen to him with your heart, Tiger."

So I listen with my heart and I begin to hear it. It's softer than a whisper, but strong.

It's all right, Grampa Peter's silent voice says. *Now they will think that they have us where they want us. They think we are caught. And we will let them think that. Then, together, we will find a way to catch them.*

CHAPTER THIRTEEN

The Bucket

The big man who caught me unclips the cell phone from his belt, flips it open, and thumbs a number.

"Stazi here," he says. "Got him."

He clicks the phone shut, slips it back onto his belt, and starts the truck.

By the time we pull onto the drive, the first light is starting to show. The catbird that lives in the blueberry bushes behind Grampa Peter's trailer is singing its greeting to the new day. And there, sitting at the picnic table in front of the trailer, is my welcoming crew.

It's not a pleasant sight. I'd seen Darby Field before, but not with the wide grin he's now wearing. It's not a friendly smile, but a fang-bearing threat.

The anticipation in his look worries me. As does the array of things he has laid out on the table. It's half the contents of Grampa Peter's tool chest. Grampa Peter is a master craftsman. He carves, does flint knapping and woodworking, and makes baskets. He also knows how to make things like survival shelters and snares—give him four feet of rope and he can catch anything in the woods from a rabbit to a bear. But I don't think that craft work or carpentry is what Darby Field has in mind for the hammer, the nail gun, the power saws, and the drills spread out in front of him. My fingers tingle as my imagination goes to work.

The two people with Field don't make me feel any more comfortable. Tip, the guy with the South Boston accent, is a little smaller than I imagined him to be. Probably no more than five feet nine and not that bulky, with jet-black hair tied back in a ponytail. He has one of those port-wine birthmarks on his left cheek, the shape and size of a potato, and his nose looks as if it's been broken a time or two. His eyes stare into mine as I am pulled out of the truck.

Louise is actually worse. There is something positively predatory about this woman's expression as she looks me up and down and licks her lips. Whatever unpleasant stuff Field has in mind for me and Grampa Peter, Louise is ready and waiting for it.

I look at Grampa Peter, who has been tied to one of the bentwood chairs he crafts to sell at the shops in Conway. His mouth isn't taped shut like mine, but he still doesn't speak out loud. He just gives me the smallest nod and presses his lips together.

I'm sorry this is happening to you.

It's okay, Grampa. I'm okay.

Stazi hooks one arm under my right elbow, drags me over to the bench that has been placed in front of Field, and sits me down.

Field reaches out and rips the tape from my face. My mouth burns and I suck in my lower lip and taste the blood. I'd cut my lip while I was rock climbing four days ago. The scab was just beginning to heal over.

"Hell-lllooo," Field says in his irritating accent. "How nice of you to drop in, young Paul." He makes an expansive gesture toward the top of the picnic table behind him. "As you can see, we have been expecting you."

I bite my tongue. I'm not going to say anything.

"Oh my, are you as mute as your grandfather?

Fear not, lad, we have our little ways of eliciting a response. But we don't need you to talk, we just need you to scream."

His open hand whips out like a rattlesnake striking as he slaps me across the face. I turn my head to look back at him. I won't give him the satisfaction of showing how scared I really am.

He chuckles. "Made of stern stuff, eh? I do like a bit of a challenge."

Field turns back to look at Louise, who is now leaning over his shoulder and staring at the blood dripping down my chin as if she wants to drink it. "Remember that chap in Colombia?"

"'Quest for the Forbidden City of Gold,'" Louise whispers.

"Was his name Martin?"

"Yes, it *was*." Her emphasis on that last word sends a chill down my back.

"He insisted that he knew nothing. But it turned out that he knew quite a bit more than he said." Field picks up a pair of needle-nose pliers and taps them against his palm. "It is truly amazing what losing a few fingernails does for one's memory."

He looks at the pliers and then shakes his head regretfully. "But we don't have time for that, do we? And I have found that sometimes

71

the most effective methods are the oldest ones. No need for modern tools at all." He tosses the pliers back onto the table and snaps his fingers.

"Tip!"

Tip leans over to pick up a big white plastic bucket, one of the empty ones that Grampa Peter has stacked up behind the trailer.

You never know when you're going to need a good bucket, I find myself thinking.

But the bucket is not empty now. It's filled to the brim with water.

Tip sets the bucket in front of me. Stazi places one of his huge hands on top of my head, and the other goes on my shoulders. He pushes down, bending me forward until my nose is almost touching the water. A single drop of my blood falls from my cut lip, strikes the surface, and then disperses in a circling red cloud through the water. I take a deep breath.

"No!" Grampa Peter says. It's probably his first spoken word since being taken captive.

Field chuckles.

"Now," he whispers.

And my head is thrust under the water.

CHAPTER FOURTEEN

Drowning

Having your head pushed underwater, even by a friend joking around in a swimming pool, can be a very unpleasant experience. Especially if you don't expect it. The situation I am in right now is a lot worse. Needless to say, the ones thrusting my head underwater are not my friends. There is no kidding around involved. Their intentions are deadly serious.

But knowing I was about to be dunked, even a split second before it happened, gave me enough time to do what I could to prepare. To plan three steps ahead of them.

The first step, taking a series of quick deep breaths before I was pushed under—packing air into my lungs—is the one I've already taken.

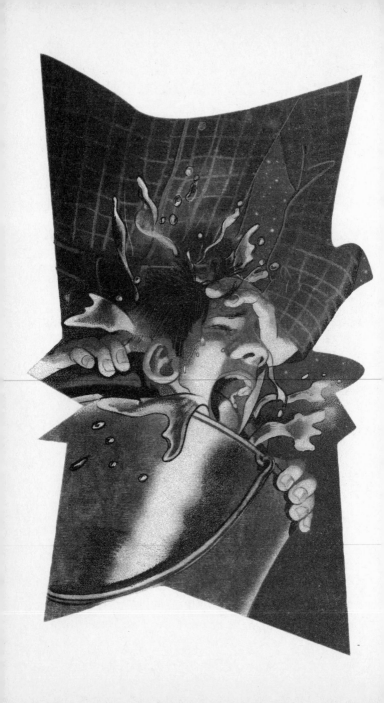

It doesn't mean I'm not in danger of being drowned, but it does give me time. I've always been able to hold my breath for a long time, so the strategy I have in mind ought to work.

Step two is to make them think I am panicking. So, even though I'm not terrified, I wave my arms and bang them against the side of the bucket as if trying in vain to lift my head out, which of course I cannot do with the meaty paw of a 250-pound East German gorilla on the back of my head.

Step three depends on my assumption that Darby Field does not want to actually drown me. His objective is to force my grandfather to do what he wants by torturing me. Actually killing me would defeat the purpose. Field wants me alive—at least for now. So, here goes step three. I stop pushing my head back against Stazi's hand, stop waving my arms. I go totally limp.

And just like that I am yanked out of the water and dropped on my side on the ground, where I lie like a limp dishrag.

"No!" Grampa Peter is yelling. "You've killed him, my poor grandson!"

It almost makes me smile. I can hear from the way he's yelling that he knows exactly what I am up to. It ought not to have been hard for him to figure it out. It would be more than a little strange if the kid who, at the age of seven, was already diving thirty feet deep to free our lures when they got stuck in our favorite fishing lake, could drown after less than a minute in a bucket. Plus the fact that he has just said more than four words in a row is a sure sign that he's acting as much as I am.

"What did you do?" Field is snarling. "Did you break his neck?"

"I do nothing," Stazi answers, his tone more than a little defensive. "I only do what you say."

I'd like to lie here and listen to their argument heat up even more, but I might start laughing if I do that. Plus any minute now someone might decide to start doing CPR. The thought of any of them giving me mouth-to-mouth is enough to turn my stomach. So I cough convulsively and spit out the mouthful of water I sucked in just before being pulled from the bucket.

Stazi pulls me up from the ground, thumping his hand on my back in an effort to be helpful. He hits me so hard that he almost knocks me down, and I start coughing for real.

"Back off, *dummkopf*!" Field pushes him away from me, steers me to the bench, and sits me down. He's trying to regain control of the situation, the movie director getting things back on script.

I sit there, wiping my face, snuffling, being the pathetic kid who has just had the scare of his life but is still trying to be brave. Out of the corner of my eye I see Grampa Peter wink at me.

"No more," Grampa Peter says. Even though he is wrapped up in more tape than a Christmas package, his voice is so strong that it turns every head toward him.

Field keeps his eyes on my grandfather, but reaches out to grab my shirt and pull me toward him, a further reassertion of control on his part.

"What's that I hear?" Field asks. "Are you ready to cooperate?"

Grampa Peter stares at him, his eyes as fierce as an eagle's. Then he nods his head.

"I will do it."

CHAPTER FIFTEEN

Old Stories

There are all kinds of old stories that our elders tell about monsters, like the story that Pmola's wings made the wind blow so hard on top of Mount Washington. One of my teachers said it was because we were superstitious back then and didn't understand science; that we made up creatures like Pmola to explain dangerous forces of nature because we didn't understand that winds are caused by temperature changes and the motion of the earth.

I kept quiet while the teacher said all that. I didn't even bother to shake my head inwardly. I just did what I usually do whenever I start hearing that sort of talk. I left the classroom. Not physically, of course. I wasn't about to end up in detention. I just drifted off into my own daydreams.

It's not that I don't believe in science. But science doesn't explain everything. My ancestors were not stupid or foolish. We had our own ways of understanding the world. Our stories taught us all kinds of useful lessons, like the lesson that we need to be careful when it comes to power. Some things—and some places—really are dangerous, and the best thing to do is to avoid them.

For example, there is this one river gorge in Vermont, near a town called Huntington. The old Abenaki name for that gorge is Place That Swallows Us, because our stories told of a monster that sucked people underwater and killed them. So we never seam there. Modern people who don't believe in or who don't know our old "superstitious" stories swim in that gorge every summer. And every three years or so some of those swimmers drown when the current catches them and sucks them under.

I am thinking about our monster stories right now as I sit next to Grampa Peter in the back of Darby Field's van. The truck that I tried to take was left behind when they picked up this van from a spot hidden even farther down the road from Grampa Peter's trailer.

The van is filled with all kinds of expensive-looking equipment. Right now,

Field is confidently narrating his plan and building the suspense for his imagined viewers as he talks to the camera about his daring to go to a forbidden place that is unknown to much of the world even though it is in the heart of one of North America's favorite hiking areas.

The camera that is focused on him is manned by Stazi, who, like everyone else in Field's gang, is both a bad guy and a member of the film crew. Stazi is Camera Two, using the small hand-held high-def camera. He's shooting in black and white, and his footage will be intercut with shots from the big camera on the tripod that is handled by Tip—Camera One. Louise is Sound. Right now she is holding a metal pole with a microphone covered in what looks like rabbit fur just over her boss's head.

We're parked at a pull-off that gives a view of Mount Washington through the window behind Field. It's a set-up shot for him to explain what this episode of *Forbidden Mysteries* is about: "The Search for Pmola, the Winged Monster of the White Mountains."

Of course, Grampa Peter and I are not in the picture. We are in the third row of seats, way far back. The cameras are in front of us in the middle of the big van, and Field is farther forward on a seat that has been turned around backward so that the panorama of the mountain view is visible though the windshield behind him. It's clear that this vehicle has been specially designed and outfitted for this sort of thing. And if anyone had any doubt about that, all they would have to do would be to read what is written in large red letters on both sides of the van: FIELD'S FORBIDDEN MYSTERIES.

I'm not really listening to all of the blather that Field is spouting about how the sightings of something called the Mothman, a strange giant headless being with wings, are very similar to the descriptions of Pmola.

"Poh-moh-lah and Mothman," he whispers. "Winged mysteries beyond our comprehension? Ancient beings, or visitors from a distant galaxy or some other dimension?"

And so on and so on. As if there was some connection between Pmola and the Mothman—which there isn't.

I'm pretty sure I know where Field is getting all this Mothman stuff from. You can find it on the Internet easy. Plus there was that goofy movie made starring Richard Gere, *The Mothman Chronicles* or something like that. I hear that Gere only takes roles like that because they pay

him a lot of money that he can then use for char-
ity—like helping Tibetan monks. The thought
of the Dalai Lama watching one of Gere's movies
and giggling makes me laugh out loud.

"Cut!" Field's angry voice brings me back out
of my daydream. He is glaring at me because my
laughter has undercut whatever excellent point he
thinks he was just making. "One more outburst
and I shall have Stazi tape your mouth shut again."
Field's face is as red as a beet, and he is tugging at
one end of his mustache as he snarls at me.

Even though I know that I'm not in a position where I should laugh, he looks so ridic-
ulous—like the corny villain in an old-time
movie threatening to tie the heroine to the rail-
road tracks—that I know I won't be able to say
anything without cracking up. So I just put my
head down as if I am scared stiff.

My apparent terror mollifies him, and he
makes a circling motion with his index finger
to his attentive crew: Start it rolling again.

Grampa Peter bumps his knee against mine.
I look over at him and understand the look in
his eyes. He is as amused as I am by Field's dog
and pony show, but he wants me to stay alert.
Don't daydream. Listen. Pay close attention.
Watch and wait.

I nod to him that I understand.

You can always learn something by listening. And even though I am totally uninterested in the load of horse manure that makes up *Forbidden Mysteries*, which is at least two steps below similar shows about extraterrestrials, strange creatures, ancient curses, and unexplainable phenomena, there are some things I would like to know.

For one, how much does Field really know about Pmola? Does he think it is just an old story made up to explain the strong winds around the mountain? How much does he know about Pmola's treasure? Does he know as much as the first Darby Field knew when he climbed to the mountaintop hundreds of years ago in a futile search for jewels? Does he know that the first Darby Field was deliberately led to the wrong place by his Abenaki guides? All that anyone is going to find on top of Mount Washington— aside from the things humans have brought up there—is bare stones and hungry wind.

From his bragging about all the research he's done on all the Abenaki families in our area, I understand better now how Field found Grampa Peter. Even though Grampa Peter always plays it down, it's common knowledge that he knows more about the mountains and the old stories than anyone else. It's also pretty widely known—and not just among Abenakis—that Grampa Peter has the special powers of *medawlinno* and knows the old ways. Field probably just put two and two together and figured that if anybody knew how to get to Pmola's treasure, it would be Grampa Peter.

As far as I know, there aren't any people outside our family who know the real role that Grampa Peter plays. You see, Grampa Peter is the keeper of a story that others might know, but a story that only he fully understands.

Lots of people can talk about Pmola and Pmola's treasure, but our family inherited the knowledge that makes that story real. That's why my father told me about Pmola and the good hunter when I was little, a tradition passed down among us Fortunes ever since that long-ago man stumbled on Pmola's cave and was granted good fortune—that hunter was our ancestor. As a result it's been a sacred trust for us ever since to guard that secret passed down from generation to generation. Of all the people in the whole world, only my grandfather knows the actual place where Pmola hid his treasure.

CHAPTER SIXTEEN

Things Could Get Worse

"Whenever you are feeling sorry for your-self, sweetheart, just remember things can always get worse."

That is one of my mom's favorite sayings. She trots it out whenever I am upset, and then she smiles. For some reason, it almost always makes me smile too. It is like another thing she says: The best thing to do when your troubles get really big is to relax and not worry about them, because they are way beyond your control.

Somebody who doesn't know my mom might think that her saying things like that means she is telling me to give up and be a quit-ter. But that's not it at all. What she is talking about is a kind of mental jujitsu, a reminder that you shouldn't wear yourself out with worry and self-pity when things are tough. Let me put it this way: If you fall into a flooded river and you are being swept downstream, you can't escape from drowning by struggling against the current. Instead, you should put the current at your back, let it carry you along, and try to angle your way toward the shore downstream. Go with the flow. Like I'm doing now.

We're driving up Base Road, the approach to the slopes of Mount Washington, which leads to the Ammonoosuc Ravine Trail that ascends to Lake of the Clouds Hut and is the shortest route up Mount Washington from the west. The views along the way are beautiful. It always touches something in me when I look out over those long vistas. The ancient mountains roll on into the distance, one range after another, with more shades of blue and green than you can have names for in English. And the rocks along the road are just as beautiful. Most people look beyond them, trying to see the long views. But I like to sit and study those big old boulders.

The sun is rising over the slope ahead of us. It's a brilliant golden ball of light, and its warmth touches my face through the window of the van.

I close my eyes to accept its blessings. *Kisos o-o.* The sun, it shines. The Giver of Life who always returns with a new day. I open my eyes and look over at Grampa Peter, who nods his head at me. I know that he, too, has just given his morning thanks to the sun. Despite the fact that we are in deep trouble, he hasn't forgotten to be grateful for another day of light and life.

Grampa Peter looks ahead again and I look at his profile. It is what some people call a classic Native American look. If you are a coin collector, you've seen a profile like his on those old nickels, the ones with a buffalo on one side and an Indian head on the other. Some have also said that his profile is like that of the Old Man of the Mountain. In case you don't know what I am talking about, let me explain who the Old Man of the Mountain is—or was. Not far from here, back to the west, is Cannon Mountain, which got its name because of a natural stone table that looks sort of like a cannon from Profile Clearing.

The three ledges at the upper end of the east cliff of Cannon Mountain looked like a huge face when they were seen from the lake and the clearing below. Mom says there is actually a story about it by an author named Nathaniel

Hawthorne, who lived way back in the nine-teenth century. Hawthorne called it "the Great Stone Face."

Anyhow, people made a big deal about the Old Man of the Mountain for years. Tourists came to take its picture, there were postcards made of it, and all kinds of stories were told—like that it was actually the face of an ancient chief who had been turned to stone because he dared to defy the Great Spirit.

Because it was made of piled rock ledges, that stone face became unstable over the long winters of freezing and thawing and looked as if it was going to fall. So the state actually tried to protect it. They poured rocks into the cracks and strapped the whole thing together with a system of cables and turnbuckles. Up close it made those rocks look sort of like King Kong when they had him tied down on display in that New York theater.

Then, a few years ago, guess what happened? Yup. The whole thing slid down the mountain, all three ledges. The Great Stone Face was gone. You can still read some of the wacky postings that went up on the Internet, like how this meant that the few remaining Abenaki people in our region were doomed because that great face had been watching over the land and protecting them (and doing a lousy job of it, considering New Hampshire is one of only two states in the entire Northeast without even one acre of reservation land). A number of officials in the state parks, and even more in the tourism industry, wanted to drag those poor rocks back up to the place where they had been and rebuild the Old Man of the Mountain.

Somehow, someone from one of the local TV channels got word about Grampa Peter, this old Indian who looked just like the famous profile and who was some sort of elder, maybe even a medicine man. They called to ask him to come with them to shoot a story about the fall of the Old Man of the Mountain. I was visiting him when it happened and I watched as he nodded his head while the voice in the phone kept talking on and on, so loudly I could hear it from where I was sitting on the couch.

When there was a pause in the conversation, Grampa Peter spoke his first words since he'd said "Hello." They were, "You gonna feed us?" When the voice on the other end assured him that we'd be taken out to lunch before the shoot, Grampa Peter said, "See you at eleven," and hung up.

The day wasn't bad. The newscaster did his intro, and then the lens was turned on Grampa Peter, who really did look pretty impressive with his long white hair around his shoulders and his brown-skinned craggy face turned just so that the mountain and its empty face were behind him. He raised one hand dramatically, his open palm gesturing toward the place where the ledges had been.

"Rocks," he said. Then he dropped his hand down and shrugged. "They fall."

That was the end of his speech. The newscaster tried to save the day by stepping in with his mike and asking one question after another. But Grampa Peter was finished with talking. All he would say in reply was "Hmmm," whenever the reporter paused in hope of an answer. Needless to say, the piece was never aired.

Remembering that almost puts a smile on my face. But then the van hits a bump and reminds me where we are as I am tossed to the side, unable to steady myself with my hands because they are taped together in front of me.

How could things get worse?

CHAPTER SEVENTEEN

A Fall

As we start to slow down, Darby Field looks at Grampa Peter.

"Where's the spot?" he asks.

Grampa Peter jerks his head to the right, pointing with his chin at a narrow pull-off on the shoulder.

"There," he says.

The van edges off the Base Road to a steep dirt track, just wide enough for a single vehicle. In only a few yards we have dropped down at least forty feet below the road, turned behind a jumble of huge boulders, and stopped at a spruce thicket. We aren't quite high enough yet to be in the alpine zone. Up there all the trees are so dwarfed by the altitude and the thin soil that a two-hundred-year-old juniper might be only ten inches tall. The spruces here are no more than ten feet high, but they provide effective cover from the road above us. The only way the van could be seen now would be from one of the higher slopes across from us or from an airplane or helicopter.

Stazi goes around the back, opens the door, and pulls out a pair of brush cutters. He goes to the front of the van and begins working on the spruces there, cutting them down and piling them to the side, creating an opening. The smell of the cut spruce branches fills my nostrils. I've always liked that scent, but it seems jarring to me right now. It also mixes with the odor of Stazi's sweat, which makes me think of the musky scent of a dangerous animal. When the big man is done, he puts the brush cutters back and opens the door next to us.

"Rausen," he says, gesturing for us to get out.

When we don't move quickly enough, he reaches in, grabs each of us by the elbow, and yanks us out as if he were unloading cargo. It's easy for him to do that because we each have our wrists taped together in front of us. I manage to keep on my feet, but Grampa Peter takes a step, stumbles, and falls to his side in front of

Field and the other two members of his crew. That surprises me. My grandfather is usually as sure-footed as a mountain goat. Did he stumble over something? I thought I saw something on the ground as we were yanked out, but there's nothing there when I look now.

Tip, who obviously still bears Grampa Peter some ill will, lets out a loud nasty laugh. "No time for a nap now." He chuckles and pulls back a foot, taking aim at my grandfather's side as if he were going to attempt a field goal. I'm about to try to throw myself in between Grampa Peter and a rib-breaking kick, but I don't have to.

"Tip!" Field steps in front of his stocky hench-man with one hand raised. "Not now."

Tip grudgingly lowers his foot and steps back. "Later, pops," he snarls.

I reach down with my taped-together hands and help Grampa Peter to his feet. It's not easy. He's almost a dead weight. His legs don't seem to want to work right. It's as if my grandfather has suddenly gone from being as strong and flexible as a man half his age to being an elderly person crippled by arthritis. When he stands up, his shoulders are stooped and his head is down.

I'm worried about him and angry at the same time. I glare at Field and Tip, who completely ignore me. Louise, though, gives me one of her predatory smiles. She's enjoying the sight of my grandfather looking like a scared and beaten old man.

Stazi has paid no attention to any of this. There's a cold, businesslike air about the way he does things. He gets back into the driver's seat and pulls the van forward into the space he has cut in the spruce thicket. Then he unloads the remaining gear from the back and begins placing the cut spruces around and on top of the vehicle. When he's done, Field's *Forbidden Mysteries* van has totally vanished from sight.

Field dusts his hands together. "Excellent," he says. "Now a bit of set-up, eh?"

He turns toward Tip and Louise, who have taken out their equipment. The camera Tip is about to use is small enough to hold in one hand. Louise's sound recorder is the size of an iPod and is clipped to her belt. The microphone she holds up is no bigger than a lollipop. Even the larger stationary camera that Stazi has produced and fastened to the top of a collapsible tripod must weigh only a few pounds.

Field nods. Then he clears his throat and gestures dramatically. "Many have perished in search of our elusive quarry," he intones. "Among them, the native elder who gave us the clues that we will follow today, and who showed us the secret path known only to his ancestors, whose feet trod these trackless wastes for untold centuries before the arrival of the first Europeans. I'll say more about his tragic fall later, about the climbing accident that took his life." Field pauses and attempts to look pensive. To me, though, he looks like a rat thinking about a piece of cheese he just ate. "Or was it an accident? We must press on without pause or trepidation. Another forbidden mystery awaits us at Pmola's Peak, where we seek the great winged creature who guards a lost treasure."

Field makes a throat-cutting gesture and looks at his crew.

"Well?" he asks.

"Perfect," Louise says, giving him a thumbs-up.

"Nailed it on the first take, boss," Tip agrees.

Stazi just grunts.

Field favors them all with one of his wide, toothy grins.

I look over at Grampa Peter. He still has his head down, and his eyes are half closed. Is he sick or hurt? Has he given up? I can't believe what I'm seeing. I've always thought of him as indestructible, like a part of the mountain itself.

The way he is standing bothers me as much as what I've just heard in Field's overblown monologue. Because if I heard it right, Field was talking about my grandfather. And the tragic fall, the so-called accident he mentioned, is not in the past but is yet to come.

CHAPTER EIGHTEEN

Off the Trail

When I was a little kid, Mom and Dad used to take me to the Abenaki shop in Conway, New Hampshire. It was a special place because it was the one spot in our state that most people thought of as really belonging to the Abenaki. Many generations of Abenaki people had sold such things as baskets and carvings and crafts on the same site, and the same family, the Laurents, had always been there. The state highway department tried to put a bypass through their land, but the Laurents had managed to stop that—with the help of their friends and neighbors, who may not have been Indian themselves, but who valued the family's gentle presence. There was even a state historical marker in front of their shop.

The stories Mr. Laurent told me whenever I visited have always stayed with me. One story in particular is going through my mind right now as we trudge along. It's about an Abenaki man who wanted to see the Manogemassak, the Little People. The Little People in our stories are kind of like those leprechauns the Irish talk about. They have special powers, and it's said that they can grant wishes. But they don't like to be seen unless they are ready to show themselves.

"I wish I could see those Manogemassak," I said to Mr. Laurent when he first told me about them. I was only five years old then.

"Ah," he said, going down on one knee. He was a very tall man, and I remember how big his hands were when he reached out and placed them on my shoulders. "There was a man who said that very thing, not long ago. He knew that the Manogemassak had a certain place by the river where they came at night. They used the clay to make pots and sometimes left little swirls of clay that people would find. So, do you know what that man did?"

I shook my head.

"That man decided he could trick the Little People. He put his canoe down by the river and left it there upside down for several days and

98

nights. When he thought those Little People must have gotten used to it, he went and hid under that canoe and waited until dark, sure he would see them and not be seen. Do you know what happened then?"

I shook my head again, even though I had a feeling, young as I was, that it was something unexpected.

Mr. Laurent smiled. "That man did not come home the next day or the next, and people went looking for him. They found his canoe right side up at the riverbank. At first they saw no sign of the man. Then someone noticed a big pile of clay, about this tall and this long."

He held a hand up to my chest and then spread both of his long arms out to either side.

"It was sort of shaped like a person. And there was a little hole in the head where the mouth would be. That clay was as solid as a rock, but when they listened at the mouth hole, they thought they could hear a faint voice saying, 'In here, in here.' They broke the clay open with rocks, and there was that man who had wanted to see the Little People. He was weak and could barely talk. They took him home, and after a few days he finally told them what had happened. As he hid under his canoe and it got dark, he began to hear soft whispering voices. Then, all of a sudden, his canoe was flipped over, and he felt little hands all over him. The next thing he knew, he was trapped inside that mound of clay."

Mr. Laurent looked down at me. "So," he said, "what do you think of that?"

I remember pausing and scratching my head. Then I looked up. "I would like to see the Little People," I said, "if they would like me to see them."

Why am I thinking of that story right now? Because as I've gotten older, I've better understood the lesson that Mr. Laurent was sharing with me. We don't have to see everything or solve every mystery. In fact, there are some things that we do not need to know, things that should be left alone.

If trying to see the Manogemassak without them wanting you to see them is a dangerous thing to do, think of how much more dangerous it is to go looking for a being as powerful as Pmola. Talk about being between a rock and a hard place!

We've been on the hidden trail for an hour now and we are way off any of the regular hiking routes. I've actually walked part of this very

trail before with my grandfather, but everything seems different today. Usually when I am
out in the woods, every step I take that leads
me away from roads and cars and the sounds
of the modern world feels like a step toward
freedom. Not so today.

And there is something else. The land around
us, even the sky above us, feels different. Do you
know how sometimes the air seems to tremble
because a big storm is coming? It's that kind
of feeling. The air has that clean, edgy scent of
ozone in it.

I look up at the sky and squint my eyes.
There's not a cloud in sight, but I think I can
see something way up there, circling. Maybe it's
an eagle. Maybe not. I know it isn't an airplane.
I actually haven't seen a single vapor trail from
a jet since we left the van hidden in that spruce
thicket, and on a clear day like today that's strange.
Commercial jets cross over here all the time, and
air force planes also use the sky over the White
Mountains. In fact, I remember one time when
Grampa Peter and I were walking a trail not
far from here and a whole group of those little
single-passenger ultralight planes came buzzing
over like lawn mowers with wings. But today
there's nothing.

Someone shoves me hard in the back.

"Move," a voice growls.

I don't have to look back to know it's Tip. He's probably hoping I'll fall down when he pushes me, like Grampa Peter did. He's itching to get a kick in on one of us when Field isn't looking. I keep my balance, even with the heavy pack on my back, and continue on up the trail.

Oh yeah, the pack: Field strapped it to me before we started on the trail. I'm not sure what it contains, but there has to be at least forty pounds of stuff in it. I'm used to backpacking, so I'm not having much trouble carrying it, though I do resent being both a doomed captive and a beast of burden. Yet another reason for me to glare at Field's broad back as he strides up the trail ahead of me, unencumbered by anything other than a walking stick.

When we set out, I'd wondered how the four of them would do hiking a trail. I sort of hoped that they'd be soft and not used to this kind of mountain walking. I imagined them stumbling and falling and getting worn out to the point where Grampa Peter and I could slip away from them.

No such luck. The four of them seem to be experienced hikers, and even Louise changed into well-worn hiking boots before we started on our trek. I guess they have all gotten toughened up by searching out forbidden mysteries in other parts of the world and gracing other indigenous people like me and Grampa Peter with their friendly presence. From what I've overheard, it sounds as if being chosen to be a guide for this group of psycho documentarians is like being invited for a swim in a shark tank. For example, one of the cliff faces we just passed reminded Louise of "the one that Quechua guy in Peru fell off when we were filming 'Lost City of Gold.'"

How have they gotten away with it? I suppose I don't have to ask that question, do I? These days the world is full of remote and dangerous places where law and order don't mean much if you are a poor, uneducated peasant. No one pays attention when one more peon meets with an unfortunate accident. Especially if the people that peasant was working for are famous and wealthy westerners.

So Field and his gang have gotten used to it, I guess. And they think it'll be just as easy to get rid of us when we are no longer useful to them. They're wrong about that. They don't know who my parents are. If anything happens to me, my mother and father won't rest until they've tracked down the people responsible for my death.

Whoa! This thought is not at all comforting. I'm already writing my own obituary. I look over at Grampa Peter, who is trudging along with his head down. He looked so old and frail before that they didn't even try to put one of the packs on his back. Field didn't want to take a chance on Grampa Peter giving out before he had showed them the way to go. So he is pretty much being left alone, aside from Field coming back to ask him at each turn in the trail which way to go and Grampa Peter lifting up his shaking, infirm, taped-together hands to point out the right direction.

I've heard about stress making people grow old overnight. About people's hair turning white from fright. Stuff like that. But I never thought I would see that in my own grandfather, who has always been as tough and resilient as an old cedar tree. Is it possible that he might be faking it?

There's a big rock across the trail. We can't go around it, because the brush is thick here on both sides. Grampa Peter is having a hard time getting up over the boulder. If my hands were not still taped together, too, I'd reach out my arm

to help him. Instead I lean my shoulder against him as a support. His foot skids on the rock and falls back against me, both of us stumbling partway off the trail into the brush. The scent of crushed cedar needles fills my nostrils, and then the smoky leather scent that always clings to my grandfather. He's landed right on top of me. I find myself looking up into his smiling face. Then I feel his hands pressing against mine. He whispers a word into my ear.

Stazi, who has been bringing up the rear of our little party, wades into the brush to pull us out. First Grampa Peter, who seems so shaken by his fall that he grabs holds of Stazi's shirt and has to be pried off. Then he has to sit down, pathetically gasping for breath as the rest of the nefarious crew comes back to make sure their antiquated guide is still capable of keeping on.

This gives me plenty of time to shove the rope that Grampa Peter passed to me into my shirt and under the waistband of my pants. By the time Stazi reaches in to extricate me from the brush, I have also managed to get the smile off my face that appeared when I realized some things. One, of course, is that Grampa Peter really has been faking this routine of being a tired old man. He's playing possum. Another is that I had indeed seen something on the ground when we were yanked out of the van. It was a coil of thin nylon rope that must have been lost by some previous hiker. And it was plenty long enough to be used the way Grampa Peter told me to with that one word he whispered.

"Snares."

CHAPTER NINETEEN

One Big Bird

"No bars."

We've stopped for our four captors to drink from their canteens. Tip is frowning at his cell phone and tapping it with an index finger.

"Tip, Tip." Field's patronizing voice comes from behind me. "You're wasting your time with that. Reception is spotty at best in mountains such as these, filled with magnetite ore. And who were you about to call?"

"Just tryin' to check my messages," Tip complains. "No law against that."

Field looks at an electronic device of his own that he has pulled from one of the many pockets in the khaki vest he put on just before we started our hike. And now he is frowning too.

"Strange," Field says to himself. He looks over at Grampa Peter as if to ask him a question, but catches himself before he does so. He's learned that even though my grandfather may look as if he is about to keel over and die at at any minute, it hasn't done a thing to loosen his tongue.

Field shoves the device in his hand in front of my face. "Know what this is, boy?"

I nod my head. "It's a GPS unit."

We see a lot of them up here. I have never used one myself. Having lived near here all my life, I don't even use a guidebook like the ones put out by the Appalachian Mountain Club. But these days most hikers and hunters and fishermen carry GPS units with them whenever they go out. On a nice day in the summer, you can sit on certain high spots that look out over the main trails and see three or four different parties of flatlander hikers walk for a hundred yards or so, then stop to check their satellite coordinates, then walk, then stop, and so on all the way up the mountain. As if they could get lost on a marked trail in broad daylight. Actually, maybe they could.

"Well?" Field snaps.

"It isn't giving you a reading," I reply.

"I know that. The question is why."

I don't know the answer to that. I understand why Field is confused. There's nothing, except for that big bird that is still circling high above, between us and the location of that geosynchronous satellite. Strange. I almost say he really should hand it to Grampa Peter, because if anyone in the world can get a piece of electronic equipment to work, it's him. But I am not about to go out of my way to be helpful. So all I say is, "I don't know much about stuff like that."

"Idiot," Field snarls. I think for a minute he is going to hit me with the GPS.

Stazi comes up just then. He's holding his own GPS unit.

"Might be sunspots. Solar flares can interfere, ja?"

"Hmmpph," Field says, then jams the GPS back into one of his pockets, turns on his heel, and almost bumps into Louise, who is looking up into the sky, shading her eyes with her palm. Why he didn't notice her behind him is beyond me. Her perfume, which smells like a mixture of rotting roses and a cat box overdue for a cleaning, is so strong that I can tell whenever she is within a hundred feet of me.

"That is one big bird," she says.

"Where?" Tip reaches into the pack he's placed at his feet. He pulls out a long-barreled machine pistol. Clearly he is one of those people who likes to shoot at anything that moves whenever he goes into the woods.

Field holds up his hand.

"No gunfire," he commands. "Too high for you to hit with that popgun anyway." He snaps his fingers. "Come on, give me the glasses."

Tip looks like a dog that's been kicked in the teeth just as it was about to bite into a bunny, but he puts the gun away and pulls out a set of binoculars.

Field lifts them up to his eyes, focuses. "Got it. Moving fast, whatever it is. Now it's diving."

He's following the dark-winged shape, but as it moves across the midday sun, he's momentarily blinded.

"Blast it!" He drops the binoculars from his eyes.

"Eagle?" Stazi asks.

"Couldn't tell," Field says, rubbing his eyes and blinking. "Sizable, though. Probably a golden eagle." Then he smirks at me. "Unless it's your fabled Poh-moh-lah."

He thinks he is being funny. But I was also watching that huge-winged creature as its flight took it across the sky. Even without binoculars I could tell that it was larger than any eagle I'd ever seen before. I also saw that the direction it was traveling led down as if it was going to land above the little pass through the rocky hills just ahead of us. The same direction we are going.

Field and Stazi and Tip and Louise are ignoring me now. They are still trying to decide whether or not to break out the cameras and "work this sighting into the narrative of their dramatic quest. They're also taking turns drinking something that has the sharp smell of alcohol from a silver flask that Stazi has just produced from his back pocket.

I look over at Grampa Peter, asking the question with my eyes. *What was that?*

He links his thumbs together, spreads his open palms wide, then nods his head.

CHAPTER TWENTY

Distant Rumble

"Right or left?" Field is talking to Grampa Peter the way you would to someone who is mentally challenged. Grampa Peter is still pretending it doesn't bother him. He keeps playing the part of the feeble old man who is so broken that he'll do whatever they ask him to do—aside from talking.

Grampa Peter nods toward the pass just above us. The way is narrow, with ridges rising and falling. The land looks as if it were made by the hands of a giant, pushing rocks together here, dropping piles of boulders there. Sometimes we're at the edge of long drop-offs and other times we're squeezing through narrow crevices.

We've stopped twice for Field to shoot more of his dumb speeches about the danger and difficulty of his quest. He's actually changed his shirt each time—making it appear as if we have been on the trail for days rather than just a few hours. If we had stayed on the regular trail, we would have been at the Lake of the Clouds Hut by now, which is only three miles from the trailhead at the end of Base Road.

We haven't run into any hikers or seen any sign of other people, even from the overlooks that give us a view of one or two of the other trails. I suppose that's not so strange. This is a vast area, and even on a beautiful summer day like this, when lots of people should be out hiking, you can avoid others by not using the easiest and most direct routes. But things feel sort of wrong to me, and I still haven't seen a plane or even heard the distant rumble of a jet from the cloudless sky.

It's really steep here, almost straight up. Tip is huffing a little, and Louise has a grim and determined look on her face as she climbs. Stazi is reaching back and helping Field, who looks a little winded. At first none of them notice what Grampa Peter and I hear at the same time. It's a rumbling, but not from the engine of a

plane overhead. A couple of pebbles fall from the rock face next to us, and then the ground begins to shake.

"Avalanche!" Stazi yells.

I look up, but only for a second. Grampa Peter grabs me by the shoulder and yanks me up onto a ledge. You'd think I weighed nothing the way he does it. Weak old man, indeed. He pushes me back, and we flatten ourselves against the cliff side as a cloud of dust filled with stones of all sizes—some of them as big as cars—comes rolling and bouncing like a huge moving curtain pulled in front of our faces. We're at just the right angle so that it is all going past us, rattling and roaring and sounding like a gigantic freight train. It's terrifying, but it's also exciting. When something dramatic like a huge thunderstorm or an avalanche happens, it reminds me of the power of nature, and it makes me feel elated. My heart is thumping in my chest.

And my mind is moving just as fast as the rock slide. I'm wondering what caused it. Did it just happen by accident, or did someone begin it on purpose by pushing a key rock that started the others rolling? What was it that I saw as I looked up at the top of the ridge? Was it a rock starting to fall or was a wide-shouldered person moving up there?

Then I think of something else. Were our four captors caught in the rock slide? Maybe this has saved us. I hate to think of anyone being killed by an avalanche, but if anyone deserved it, they did.

The dust from the slide is so thick that it is getting into my eyes and my nose and my throat. I'm racked with coughs, finding it hard to keep my balance on this narrow ledge. But if I slip off it, I'll be carried away by the avalanche and killed for sure. Grampa Peter and I are holding on to each other and keeping each other steady, pushing a little, pulling a little, readjusting ourselves almost like two dancers, preventing each other from falling. I'm remembering something my dad told me, about how grandparents and grandchildren are even closer to each other on the circle of life than kids and their parents are. Grandparents and grandchildren support each other.

Suddenly the noise stops except for a ringing in my ears and an increasingly distant rumble from below that ends as the last rocks hit the bottom.

Grampa Peter and I help each other off the ledge and look below. What there was of a trail is gone. At one point, just a hundred feet below, the ledge has been sheered off and there's a straight drop. Going back down the way we came is out of the question. But we can keep climbing up.

"I think we can cut across and get to one of the main trails beyond the ridge above us," I say.

Grampa Peter nods and I smile at him.

"We're safe, Grampa. Now we just have to get this tape off our wrists."

"I vould say no," a deep voice rumbles from behind me. I turn to see Stazi's large, square head rising from the other side of the boulder that sheltered him from the avalanche. There's a long gash on his cheek that is dripping blood, but aside from that he seems uninjured.

And just to add to this turn of bad luck, three other figures appear behind him. Field, Louise, and Tip, who is actually holding his camera and has clearly managed to film some of the near disaster. Like Stazi they are dusty and bruised, but still in possession of their lives, their packs, their weapons . . . and us.

CHAPTER TWENTY-ONE

Fabled Monsters

Things have gone from bad to worse. It's night now, and we are still on the mountain. Just where I am not sure. Ever since the avalanche I haven't been sure of much of anything. Other than the fact that my grandfather is trickier than a raccoon. Of the six of us, he is the only one who is totally relaxed and unconcerned right now. Not that Field and his gang know that. They think he is unconscious and maybe dying.

After Stazi pulled us down from that ledge, Grampa Peter started acting strange. Matter of fact, he also looked weird. He looked fine just before I was yanked down from my perch and lost sight of him for a second. But then I heard

Stazi say, "Vat is wrong *mit* you?" and I turned around to see my grandfather, his face covered with blood, fall into the big man's arms.

I had to help Stazi carry him—which was not easy with my wrists taped together—to where the other three were still collecting themselves. Grampa Peter was moaning, his fingers opening and closing, and every now and then his whole body would shake as if he was going into convulsions.

"Grampa," I kept saying. "Don't die, Grampa. Don't die!" Tears were flowing out of my eyes and I was sobbing.

I probably would have meant it if I hadn't caught the little hand gesture he gave me as I was picking him up. His ring finger and his little finger briefly extended and moved twice in a circle.

Keep it going, play along with me.

So I did. And the crying part was easy since I still had so much dust in my eyes that they were watering like crazy.

Darby Field was so upset I thought he was going to hit Stazi.

"I told you to keep an eye on the old man," Field yelled, waving his arms, his eyes bulging like they were going to pop out of his head.

Stazi stared at him. "So," he said in a slow voice, "you vant I should haf let you be crushed by der rocks?"

That stopped Field's yelling. But he turned around and started to take his anger out on Tip, who cringed in front of him like a dog that's used to being kicked. The only one who didn't get all that worked up about my grandfather's condition was Louise. She was busy fishing in her fanny pack for a mirror and a comb and some other stuff to repair her makeup. One cold customer.

I'd managed to get some tissues out of my pocket to wipe my grandfather's face. I could see what he'd done, just spread the blood from a scalp wound in the hair above his forehead. It wasn't a bad cut, but scalp wounds bleed a lot. I didn't let on that it wasn't serious, just dabbed it out of his eyes and then smeared the blood and dust around a little more on his cheeks so that he ended up looking worse.

The others soon realized that there was no way to go back down the mountain. It had to be onward and upward. But without a clear trail, it took us a long time to pick our way through the maze of rocks, plus we had to be careful not to dislodge any stones that might start another slide.

Stazi and Tip were assigned to Grampa Peter. They held him up on either side as he weakly tried to walk. Most of the time they were pretty much carrying him along. In little ways, stumbling now and then, going limp at others, almost toppling backward, my grandfather made himself as heavy a load as you could imagine. And all the while he kept moaning—not words, just sounds like, "Unnnh, oooohh, hunnnh, hunnnh." Tip looked ready to have a heart attack himself, and even Stazi was exhausted by the time we reached the top of the ridge above the slide.

"If," Tip panted, "he doesn't . . . actually die . . . I am gonna kill him."

They let go of my grandfather's arms, and he slumped down onto all fours. I dropped down next to him.

"Grampa," I said. "Grampa!" I managed to keep my voice all concerned, even after he lifted his head just enough for me to see him lift both eyebrows up and down a couple of times like Groucho Marx in one of those old movies Grampa Peter is always watching on Turner Classic Movies.

The trail led back down again from the ridge to what looked like a good place to camp. There was a flat area in a grove of trees and also a brook.

Was it Monroe Brook? If so, there was a waterfall near here and a pool. I should have known this spot, but it looked, well, different. And I didn't remember the trees being that big around here.

Field's crew had come prepared for at least one night of emergency camping. They had a couple of tents, sleeping bags, one of those mini cooking stoves, pots, and packets of freeze-dried food. Most of the heavier stuff, in fact, was in the pack I'd been forced to carry.

It was getting dark by the time the campsite was set up, including a ring of stones where they made a campfire and started boiling the water they had me lug from the brook for them. In the old days you could always drink the water straight from the streams up here, but since the last part of the twentieth century, even the high mountain streams had become unsafe to drink because of coliform and a parasite that causes something called beaver fever. Which is a lousy name for it since it actually comes from human waste contaminating the streams, not beavers.

For some reason, though, as soon as I bent over that stream and smelled its water, I found myself leaning down, cupping my bound hands, and drinking. It tasted clean and sweet.

Anyhow, here we are now like a bunch of happy Boy Scouts, sitting around the campfire and about to sing songs together. Not.

My grandfather is conked out next to me with a blanket over him. I found a place where the moss was really thick and managed to maneuver us both into that spot. The best place for sleeping, even if it isn't close to the fire. Neither of us have sleeping bags—those are reserved for Field and company. We just have a couple of thermal blankets. It won't bother us, though. We are both used to spending the night in the woods with even less than this. We were also handed a little food—not much, but enough to give us the energy we'll need tomorrow to do some more walking.

Field must have thought ahead enough to plan for a situation something like this because he brought along a couple of combination locks and the kind of plastic-encased cables that are used to secure a bicycle. We each have a cable looped tightly around our right ankles connecting us to the spruce tree that arches overhead.

"You think the old man is going to be up to it tomorrow?" Louise asks.

It's dark, but I see Field's teeth reflecting the firelight as he grins. "He had better be. If not, we have our methods." Field chuckles, and a chill runs down my back. I can imagine what those methods might be. When they unpacked their gear and I saw the needle-nose pliers and the heavy-duty metal cutters, my imagination started working overtime. I find myself curling my hands in, reflexively protecting my fingers and my nails.

"Boss?" Tip's voice is tentative.

"Yes, Tip." Field's tone is that familiar condescending one. "What now?"

"Boss, I was just thinking."

"A dangerous pursuit for one so ill-prepared," Field drawls.

"Huh?" Tip sounds confused.

Louise laughs, and I can see by the motion of his silhouetted form against the fire that Tip turns to glare at her.

Field sighs. "Ah, Tip, Tip, if you must share some gem of perception with us, do it now."

"Okay, I will. I think I saw something."

"As we all have done often in our lives," Field replies.

Louise snickers even louder, but this time Tip ignores her.

"No, I mean before those rocks started coming down the hill. I saw something. It was up on the hilltop and it was like . . ."

Tip pauses. Whatever he wants to say, he's having a hard time getting it out.

Field gives another sigh. "Out with it, Tip. I assure you that I am listening, no matter how inane or insane your little insight might be. I am . . . here for you."

Tip takes a deep breath and then lets it out in a rush of words. "Okay. What I saw looked like it was a giant . . . with wings."

I take a deep breath of my own. Field and Stazi are now laughing. Tip is hunching his shoulders like someone who has just had a bucket of ice water poured over his head. I feel my grandfather's elbow dig into my side. He hasn't been sleeping at all. And he's letting me know that his reaction to what Tip just said is like mine.

Take what he says seriously.

When the laughter dies down, Field clears his throat. "Tip, forgive us for our outburst. But allow me to ask you a question or two."

Tip shifts in his seat, trying to regain his dignity. "Okay," he says after a moment. The tone of his voice is wounded.

"How many of these little expeditions have we been on together in search of our"—Field pauses dramatically—"forbidden mysteries?"

Another pause. Tip is mentally counting. "Twelve," he finally says.

"Yes. And this is number thirteen. Good. Now, exactly how many fabled monsters—apart from innuendo, and by that I mean just suggesting we might have found something with shadows, quick cuts, camera angles, and plain old fakery—how many monsters have we actually found and put onto film?"

Tip's answer is quick this time. "None."

"Excellent. But what have we found? No, let me answer my own question, Tip. We have found excellent cable ratings and sizable sales of our DVDs. And we have also found some other bonuses that we have not shared with our credulous and adoring public."

Field leans back and spreads his hands out wide, then begins to hold his fingers up one by one as he tallies their accomplishments.

"Take Ghana, for example. Did we find Sansibonsa, the ten-foot-tall forest cannibal with feet that face backward? No. What did we find?"

"Gold," Tip says.

"And in Sierra Leone, did we discover the lair of the Leopard Men? Not at all. But what did we bring home with us?"

"Diamonds," Tip replies. His voice is a lot happier now.

"And, as you well know, I could continue this little list. No fifty-foot-long lizard, but a nice take of emeralds from Australia. No vampires in the Yucatán, no giant sloth in Patagonia, et cetera, et cetera, but a very nice payoff each time. And that was not luck, Tip, but the result of careful research, separating out mere myth and folktale from the real truth: namely, that certain monsters have been invented by local folk to keep outsiders away from their little treasure troves."

Field drops his hands. "And this Poh-moh-lah is just that. A boogeyman designed to keep away those who might find that which has been hidden. A story passed down in certain families such as theirs"—Field points back in our direction—"to protect their little heirlooms."

"Like those pretty gold statues we got in Colombia," Tip says, wanting to show that he's understood what his boss is saying.

"Exactly. Of course their owners didn't know the true worth, seeing them as icons, sacred talismans that would—how did they put it, Louise?"

"Preserve the heart of the world," Louise answers, a phony tone of reverence in her voice.

"Quite. As opposed to their much greater value on the antiquities black market."

I'm clenching my fists hard now. The thought of what Field and his crew have been doing all over the world makes me wish that Pmola really is here and really was the one who started that avalanche. Field's words, though, have reassured his jumpy henchman.

"Okay, boss," Tip says. "I was just imagining things. You're right. But now I gotta go . . . you know."

"By all means," Field replies.

Tip picks up a flashlight and heads in the direction of the path that leads up out of this little valley. I hear his feet crunching the twigs and kicking against the stones. He's about twenty yards away now. Suddenly the sound of his walking stops. And the night is torn by his terrified scream.

CHAPTER TWENTY-TWO

In the Night

The scream is so loud that it makes all three of the people sitting around the fire jump up. Field, in fact, takes a stumbling step forward into the flames, knocking over the pot and producing a string of curses from him as the hot water scalds his legs. Louise and Stazi recover first. Louise shines her light in the direction of the scream, although she doesn't show any inclination to leave the fire or help. It's Stazi who bounds off into the night with an agility that is surprising for someone so large. More like some big animal than a human.

To be honest, I wasn't shocked by that scream. I'm not sure why, but something in me had been expecting it. Was it a kind of gut feeling that we were being observed? Or was it something else? And then I realize what it was. I've always had a really strong sense of smell. And I'd started smelling something as the darkness deepened. There was an unfamiliar scent on the air, almost like the musky odor of a weasel, although stronger.

I feel Grampa Peter's hands touch my elbow, and I know he is reacting the same way I am. He leans his head close to mine and whispers a word in my ear.

"Kina." Listen.

And I do. I listen beyond Field's complaining voice as he slaps at his legs. Beyond the soft thumping of Stazi's feet as he lopes toward the place where Tip just screamed. But I don't hear it yet, the sound I think I'm going to hear. Instead there is a sort of whimper, then Stazi's voice saying, "Get up," and the sound of two people coming back toward the fire, one with feet that are unsteady and stumbling.

Louise has been tossing more wood onto the fire. Now it is flaring up so high that it is casting a light well beyond the tents, even illuminating the place where Grampa Peter and I are tethered to the spruce tree. Not that anyone is paying any attention to us.

Stazi emerges, one arm around Tip's shoulders. Tip is hugging himself. He is so hunched over that he looks almost as if he's shrunk in size. They sit him down on a log by the fire.

"What in the name of heaven was that scream about?" Field yells at him.

Tip doesn't even lift his head. He just sits there on that log, clutching his shoulders and shivering.

"Give the man a drink," Louise says in a sarcastic voice. "That's always loosened his tongue before."

Her words actually get Tip to raise his head for a minute to give her a nasty look. Then he grabs the flask that Stazi is holding out to him and tips it into his mouth. It looks as if he intends to chug the whole thing, but Stazi pries it out of his hand after a couple of gulps.

Field gets down on one knee in front of Tip. "What was it?" he says, his tone of voice almost neutral for a change. "What frightened you? Did you run into a bear?"

Tip mumbles something. Field's reaction to it shows that empathy is not part of his emotional arsenal. He slaps Tip hard across the face.

"Speak up!"

To my surprise, the slap actually seems to jolt Tip back into something like his old self. Maybe this kind of mean treatment is so familiar to him that it's reassuring. He lifts his head to look at his boss and speaks more clearly.

"It wasn't a bear," he says.

"What," Field says, speaking very slowly, in the sort of way you'd ask a question of someone who was mentally deficient, "was . . . it?"

"It was big," Tip replies. Then, speaking more quickly, as if sensing he is about to get slapped again, "bigger than a bear. It towered over me. And it was black, blacker than anything I ever seen before, and it had broad shoulders." Tip holds his arms out as wide as he can. "Like this."

"Oh my," Field sighs. "Tip, Tip. Who would have thought that there was that much room for imagination in your cretinous temporal lobes?"

"Huh?" Tips says.

Field turns away from him toward the other two and then strokes his mustache. "Bear," he says in a matter-of-fact, know-it-all voice. "Drawn by the smell of our cooking, no doubt. Made to seem twice as large by his fear and the darkness. It likely turned tail and ran when our boy Tip squawked like a wounded duck."

"No," Tip says. His voice is louder than it was before. "It was no bear. Look!"

He opens his arms to point at his chest. Two slashes have been cut to make an *X* across his down jacket. Not deep enough to reach the flesh, but even with the small feathers beginning to spill out, I can see that those cuts are as clean and precise as if they'd been made with a razor.

"It done this with one finger," Tip says, pulling at the slashed fabric. "And that's not all. You know what else?"

He looks defiantly at the others, waiting for them to say something. When silence is his only reply, he answers his own question.

"It spoke to me." His voice has gotten shaky again. "It spoke to me. It said, 'Go Away!'"

Grampa Peter squeezes my arm again. And I hear what I'd been expecting now, though the four stunned people around the fire don't notice it at all. It is soft and comes from overhead, gradually growing quieter as it moves away from us.

Whomp, whomp, whomp, whomp.

It is the sound of wings. Wings bigger than those of any eagle or owl. Wings in the night.

CHAPTER TWENTY-THREE

The Edge

I'm standing with my back to the edge of the cliff. Although the full moon is bright enough to cast shadows, its light cannot illuminate the depths below. But I know that it is a long way down. My last shuffling step as I walked backward dislodged a fist-sized stone. I almost lost my balance when my heel caught it. Instead, the stone rolled back over the edge and fell and fell while I found myself counting in my head. *One, two, three, four, five, six, seven . . .* And only then, from far below, came the sound of it cracking against the sharp boulders at the bottom of the precipice.

A huge shape looms over me, its wings— as black as its eyes—spread wide, its claws glittering like obsidian razors. Its unblinking stare is focused right on me, its muzzle like that of a huge dog, with teeth in sharp, even rows like those of a bat.

There's no place to run or hide. I'm trying to figure out if there are any words that might make a difference, words that I can say to the old one that is gazing down at me the way a snake might stare at a mouse.

What was it that my mom said to me about the way a soldier behaves when there's no escape? Stay calm. Don't beg for your life. Be honest. I take two slow, deep breaths.

"Old one," I say in Abenaki, "I did not choose to come here."

Pmola leans closer. I smell its rank breath. "But you are here." Its voice echoes inside my head as a long, taloned hand reaches for me.

I open my eyes. Pmola is gone. I am back on that bed of moss next to my grandfather, who is snoring softly. I'd thought I was so hyped up that I couldn't possibly fall asleep. But I remember now that the last word my grandfather whispered to me was *"Oligawi."* Sleep good. And I did, even if I didn't dream good.

I'd have to be a total idiot not to understand the message in that dream. *Get out of here!*

But how?

It will be morning soon. The only light is still that of the moon and the distant stars, but I can sense that dawn will soon be breaking over the ridges to the east of us. Despite what happened during the night, what Tip saw or thought he saw, Darby Field and his crew decided to press on. We're only a "look" away, as distance was always measured in these mountains by my Abenaki elders. From here you can see the peak that is their destination, near Small Lake of the Clouds. That's where my grandfather told them Pmola's treasure is hidden. It's a steep climb, taking us above the tree line, but it won't take them more than an hour or two.

If we get there and they find what they are looking for, I have no doubt about what will happen to Grampa Peter and me. On the other hand, if what I think is there is waiting for them, then I have a good idea of what will happen to *all* of us.

What to do?

"Listen." Grampa Peter says that word so softly into my ear that I doubt even a bat could hear it if it was more than an arm's length away. And speaking of quiet, I hadn't even realized that he'd stopped snoring and sat up. That's how silently he moves. I don't know how I managed to keep from jumping when I felt his warm breath against my ear a half second before he spoke.

I listen. And with fewer words than you'd think would be necessary, he tells me what we need to do. Because I have long, strong legs and can run faster than him, I have a certain part to play. He has another.

I start to ask him about how we are supposed to free our hands, but when I raise them up I notice something. The duct tape has been cut through, probably while I was sleeping. My wrists are no longer fastened together.

I hold out my hands. "How?" I whisper. Maybe a little too loud.

Grampa Peter grabs my collar to pull me back close to him. He gives me a little shake and then whispers into my ear, "No Lakota."

It is everything I can do to keep from laughing. He's just told me a silly joke in two words. The word *hau*, which sounds just like *how*, is the Lakota Sioux word for "hello." Here we are in deadly danger, and he is indulging in corny Indian humor.

Some people who do not know our family well think my grandfather is a little crazy, because he has this tendency to laugh at very strange times. Some of his old Marine buddies told my dad that Grampa Peter would even start chuckling and telling rapid-fire jokes when he was in combat in Vietnam and the Vietcong were coming over the wire. But humor is a great thing if you can use it to slow down your pounding heart, to calm your fears, to make you focus in a situation where other people would be lost in panic. To be able to laugh in the face of peril, of absolute evil, is actually a very powerful thing.

So I play along and say "How?" again, but in Abenaki.

This time he gives me a straight answer.

"Houdini," he whispers.

He holds out his hand. There's a box cutter blade in it. Its edge glints in the moonlight. He holds up his left foot and shows me how the heel of his shoe pivots out when you press it a certain way to disclose the secret hollow where he had the blade hidden. Just like his hero Houdini always had lock picks and other little devices concealed on his person, my grandfather was prepared. I shouldn't be surprised. After all, one of the old traditions among our Abenaki people is that no one can ever bind or tie down a real medicine man. Which is why my grandfather sometimes says that Houdini could have been an Abenaki.

Grampa Peter hands me the blade. He doesn't have to whisper anything when he does that. I know what he is silently saying to me.

You know what to do with this.

I nod.

CHAPTER TWENTY-FOUR

Back

Have you ever been walking through the woods and come upon what seems to be a wounded partridge, stumbling away from you with one wing flopping loose, as if it is broken? Naturally you walk toward it. If you're a kindhearted person, it's because you want to see if you can help it somehow. If you're a hunter—and not a particularly bright one, I might add—then maybe you see it as an easy bird to catch for your dinner.

But just when you are almost ready to grab it, that bird flutters up and staggers a little farther away, maybe dragging its other wing this time. That is when, if you are a smart hunter, you catch on. In fact, if you know anything about the behavior of mother birds, you haven't even tried to catch it because you know it is trying to lure you away from its brood of little ones, which are hiding in the bushes in the opposite direction from the one that Mama has been trying to get you to go.

That's my job. Lure them away. It's going to take precise timing for them to not catch on to what I'm doing. I've been sitting here, just at the edge of the clearing, waiting for the right moment. Not that I haven't already been real busy. I made good use of that box cutter blade before bringing it back to Grampa Peter.

Why didn't the two of us just make a break for it, try to put as much distance as possible between us and Field's gang? We could have done that, maybe even gotten away before they caught up with us. But there's a good chance that we would not have made it. And even if we did get away, they might have decided not to chase us but to head to their original destination. And that is something that neither Grampa Peter nor I want to see happen.

There is another reason why Grampa Peter and I are doing things this way. We both have a feeling that unless we do try to stop them, unless we keep them from Pmola's treasure, we will never find our way home again. Because as soon as we set out on that trail yesterday, our journey took a turn that it is going to be hard for you to believe.

We went back in time.

Grampa Peter explained that to me. "We're not just up," he said, holding up his index finger and then pointing it over his shoulder. "We're back."

It made sense to me. That is why we haven't seen any airplanes or other hikers. That's why their cell phones couldn't get a signal and their GPS units couldn't make contact with the satellite. Where we are now, there aren't any. It also explains what I saw just a little ways back when I was making my preparations. After I'd crept away from our sleeping captors and was out of earshot of them down the trail, just before I got to those trees that were the right size, I startled a little herd of some hoofed animals that were sleeping for the night. They took off down the hill, but not before I got a real close look at their broad horns and the white and cream color of their coats. They were caribou—animals that have been extinct in northern New England for over a century.

To understand what I'm saying or to even begin to get close to believing it, you have to think a little bit like an Indian. Not a modern-day Indian whose head is totally into the European reality that has been piled up on top of this continent like landfill over a wetland, but a Native person who still remembers and believes in the wisdom of our old people. To us, time is not a straight line, and the past is never left behind. Instead, everything is a circle, and things keep happening again and again. Like the turn of the seasons or the movement of the earth around the great sun that makes day and night, day and night in an endless cycle.

I'm not talking about time travel, like in those corny movies when someone goes back in a machine or a souped-up car and does things that change the present and the future. I'm talking about stepping into a past that is always with us, a past that was then and is also now, where the flow and the balance remain unchanged. You won't meet yourself as a little kid or see your own great-grandparents, but you will—if you're Indian—find yourself in the ancient reality, the old earth that your ancestors knew. It's always been there and it will always be there.

Those old beings, like Pmola, are at the edge of European reality. They're just stories to most people. But, as my mom explained to me once, they make sense to those of us who don't see life in black-and-white terms. If you can't find Sasquatches, for example, maybe it isn't because they are just a legend. Maybe it is because they live most of the time in that other reality, the one that flows between past and present. They know the trails that lead back and forth between then and now. And our old Indian people knew those trails too. Sometimes we would only follow them in our dreams. But other times we could walk there on our feet. We could travel in ways most white people don't think possible.

I've been listening carefully. I can no longer hear my Grampa Peter making his way along the trail opposite this one, the trail that leads upward. I can hear the sounds from the three tents, though.

I can hear Tip tossing and turning, talking to himself in the midst of the nightmares he's having. I'm pretty sure I know what they are about. I can hear Darby Field snoring, making as much useless and irritating noise in his sleep as he does when he is awake. Louise, in her little tent, makes a sound as she sleeps, too. But it is more like a big cat purring than a snore. The quietest sleeper is Stazi. He's the one I am most worried about. He already caught me once, and if anyone knows enough to figure out what I am up to, it's him.

The first light is just turning the clouds red and gold, coloring the hills to the west. It's time. Darby Field has turned over and stopped snoring. He's starting to wake up. I take my position next to the tree where we were tied. We've left the little piece of metal that Grampa Peter used to pick the lock still in place in the key slot.

"Run, Grampa!" I hiss in a harsh whisper that is plenty loud enough to be heard. Then I take a few clumsy steps and deliberately fall on the ground the way someone would who's been tied for a long time and whose legs are half asleep and whose hands are duct-taped together.

"What!" The yell from Field's tent tells me he's heard just what I wanted him to hear. He pokes his head outside in time to see me get back to my feet and start running awkwardly toward the trail down the hill, my hands held up in front of me as if they were still secured by tape.

I don't have to look back to see what is going on behind me: Field staring at the place where we both were tied, seeing the picked lock. The other three come out of their tents, Tip stumbling, Louise as lithe as a panther, and Stazi already fully dressed with his boots on his feet and the look of a hunter in his eyes. I am out of their sight and running for real now, vaulting over rocks, scooting around boulders, but I am not too far away to hear Field's bellow.

"Get them!"

And then the sound of thudding feet in pursuit.

CHAPTER TWENTY-FIVE

Trip

I could lose them if I wanted to. They're not used to running in the mountains, and I've been doing this my whole life. But leaving them behind is the last thing I want to do now. I have to keep them following me.

I'm far enough ahead to risk looking back. It's not the blocked trail that we took to get up here, nor is it the one that they'd planned to follow toward Small Lake of the Clouds. That's the trail Grampa Peter is on now, hoping that no one will come after him on it soon enough to catch up. The trail that I'm on leads down into the gorge where the brook cuts through and there's a spectacular waterslide ending in a deep pool. If they're able to follow me that far, I have a plan—sort of.

I make sure I am visible from below and that I am sitting holding my wrists together as if they were still connected by the tape. I also put an exhausted and discouraged look on my face. The first one to come into sight is Stazi. Of course he notices me right away. His eyes are scanning back and forth, up and down, trying not to miss anything. That is not good.

I make like I can't see him and that I've sort of fallen down exhausted. Out of the corner of my eye I see him nod and then disappear out of sight. He'll reach the place where I am soon. I can't wait here much longer. But I want to see if the other two are still on my trail.

A voice drifts up from down below. "Hurry up." There's such cold command in Louise's tone that I wonder why she's content to take orders from Field.

"I'm goin' as fast as I can," Tip complains.

Although Stazi is out of sight from me, he must be where he can hear or see them because he calls down to Louise.

"Only der boy," he shouts. "Der old man must have gone anudder vay."

"I'll go back and tell Darby," Louise calls up to him. "You and Tip get the kid."

Only two of them after me now. But that's

enough. Sounds of feet scrabbling on the rocks of the trail are too close for comfort. I jump up and start running again.

Downhill the trail cuts into a valley where layers of soil have been trapped and there's enough shelter from the wind for some trees to grow. The path goes between two of those trees, cedars as thick as a man's forearm. I leap high as I pass between them, fly a good eighteen feet through the air, and land to take a few stumbling steps and fall down so that I'm on my side and looking back over my shoulder.

Stazi is closer than I thought he'd be. Less than twenty yards behind me, he's seen my leap and he slows to a walk, stops before he gets to the cedars. He looks down at the bicycle cable that had been used to tether Grampa Peter and me to the tree. Takes note of how I stretched it between the two trees at just the right height to trip someone running down the path. An unpleasant smile comes over his wide face.

"Good try," he says to me. His deep voice is self-satisfied.

I am hoping he'll just step over the wire or go around the trees to either side. That's where I've set three different snares with the nylon cord Grampa Peter shoved into my hands back at the van. I cut the rope into pieces with his knife blade, each one long enough to make a single snare. Not the kind you see in movies where it snatches someone up into the air upside down. I didn't have time enough for something elaborate like that, much less a big enough tree. But a small snare can catch a man's ankle and make him fall.

Stazi, though, is either smart, suspicious, or vain enough to want to outdo my impressive leap. He backs up, takes a run, and leaps as high and far as I did to land right where I'd been on the ground. Not that I am there anymore. As soon as I saw him start to back up, I got to my feet and sprinted down the trail. But I look back over my shoulder in time to see Stazi land as lightly as a cat.

"Tip," I hear him shout, "vatch out for der trip wire!"

What I do next has to be done just right. My heart is thudding, my breath coming hard as I pound uphill. I'm no longer pretending that my hands are bound. I can hear Stazi behind me, getting closer. Maybe ten strides behind. He's not going to give up now.

The stream is just ahead, over the rise and about forty feet downhill. The wall of brush

151

I piled in the moonlight has obscured it from sight, though. I crest the rise, start down. I have to jump higher and farther than I've ever jumped before.

I take a deep breath, think about the flight of an eagle, then launch myself. I go up, up, and over. My right foot ticks the highest twig of the brush wall, but doesn't catch, doesn't slow me down. I land on the other side of the stream, roll, and come up on one knee.

I'm just in time to see Stazi's huge body almost blot out the sky as he, too, comes sailing over the brush. But not as high as I did. Both of his feet tangle in the branches that I tied together near the top with the remainder of the nylon cord. It slows him just enough that instead of landing on my side of the brook, he lands hard in the shallow water on his back. He doesn't seem to be hurt because he immediately tries to get up to his knees. But the smooth rocks of the creek are slippery here. His feet go out from under him. He's on his back again, out of control. The swift flow of the water and the forty-five-degree angle of the trough he's landed in are carrying him down the long, long slide. There's no way he's going to keep from going all the way down to the pool two hundred feet below.

I stand up as I watch him going faster and faster. That's when I see it. It hadn't been visible in the moonlight. At the bottom of the slide a dead tree has lodged. Not that big a tree, but its broken branches look like short spears. Stazi can't avoid hitting it. I close my eyes, but I hear the crashing thud and a throaty cry of pain even above the noise of the rushing water.

When I open my eyes, I can see, to my relief, that the worst didn't happen. He's not dead. The way he is dragging himself out of the water, though, his left leg seems to be broken. He looks up and his eyes find mine, two hundred feet above him. His gaze is dark and expressionless. He is reaching into his coat. Maybe he's looking for something to use as a bandage. Then I see the glint of metal and drop to my belly. A dozen bullets from Stazi's pistol ping off the stones where my head had been. I crawl backward, keeping way out of sight. Any thoughts I had of trying to go down there and help him are gone.

Now I only have Tip to worry about. Or maybe not. I cross the creek and make my way quietly back to the place where I'd set my snares. I hear something even before I get there. Someone is "exercising their Anglo-

154

Saxon vocabulary," as Mom puts it, using a few curses I've never heard before. I peek around a big lichen-covered rock carefully, just in case Tip has his gun out. No worries there. Tip stepped into one snare with his left foot, and when he tripped and fell, both of his outstretched arms were caught in a second snare even more neatly than I could have planned. He is stretched out between the two snares, and the more he struggles, the tighter the little nooses get.

I come out from behind the rock and walk over to him.

"Hi," I say.

His response, which begins "You little . . ." is less than friendly, but I don't take it seriously. I just take note of the fact that not only has his pistol fallen out of his jacket pocket, so too has a small roll of duct tape. By the time I am done, I've used all the tape and Tip's wrists are even more tightly connected than Grampa Peter's and mine had been. Also, his one formerly free ankle is taped to the base of one of those cedar trees. He doesn't look comfortable, but I did the best I could under the circumstances.

I have to admit that I am feeling pretty satisfied with myself. I know that Grampa Peter and

I still have Darby Field to contend with, but this is a really good start.

I'm almost whistling as I make my way down the hill past the lookout point where I saw Stazi and heard Louise yell up to him that she was going back.

Or so she said. The thought comes to me just as I feel something hard pressed against the back of my skull and a thin, muscular arm snakes around my throat.

CHAPTER TWENTY-SIX

No Funny Stuff

A minute ago I was feeling like a hero. Now, though, I am certain that I'm a zero. Why did I think I could succeed against these people? One gawky thirteen-year-old Abenaki kid against a bunch of experienced psychopaths? This makes twice that I've been caught by one of them when I thought I had things all figured out. It just proves what my dad told me about combat: expect the unexpected.

Louise raps the right side of my skull with the barrel of her gun. It sends a jolt of pain like electricity through my head. I feel blood start to flow through my hair from the gash that the gun sight has made in the thin skin of my scalp.

"Hold your hands up, palms out, and hook your thumbs together," she says. "Now turn around."

I do as she says. I'm about five inches taller than her, so when I look at her I am looking down. She has to reach up to grab the hair on the back of my head. But that makes it easier for her to jam the gun barrel up under my chin.

There's a smile on her face, and it's probably not just from feeling satisfied about fooling me the way she did. She's enjoying the pain she's causing. She licks her lips and shows her teeth as if she is thinking of going for my throat like some kind of vampire. There's a far-off look on her face like you see in movies just before some character transforms from a human into a monster.

She shakes her head as if to wake herself from a trance, lets go of my hair with her left hand, and yanks Tip's gun out of my waistband.

"Where's Tip?" she asks, holding up his gun. The tone of her voice isn't worried, not as if she cares anything at all about him.

"He's busy," I answer. "All tied up."

She clonks me across the left temple with Tip's gun. This time she does it almost gently. I'll have a bump, but I don't think she's broken the skin.

"Funny boy," she says in that emotionless voice of hers. "And Stazi?"

I shouldn't give her a wise guy answer, but that is all my brain seems capable of right now. "He fell and he can't get up," I reply.

Louise lifts up the gun to slug me again, then thinks better of it. Maybe the fact that I don't flinch doesn't make it seem rewarding to her.

"You and your grandfather have been more trouble than you're worth," she says. She steps back and looks me up and down. "If I didn't think Darby still needed you to make sure the old bat takes him where he wants to go . . ."

She rubs her chin with the barrel of Tip's gun while she keeps her gun trained on me. "I could still put a round into you someplace where it wouldn't interfere with your walking," she says slowly. "Perhaps your shoulder?"

Although her words are being spoken aloud, I can tell by her tone that she's talking to herself, sort of thinking out loud. Trying to make up her mind about what to do, the two choices being equal. Shoot me or not.

This time I keep my mouth shut. No smart-aleck remarks that might make her decide to teach me a lesson.

"Turn back around," Louise says. "Start walking. And no funny stuff."

I bite my lip and don't say anything, even though I almost answer, "What, no more jokes?"

But with her finger on the trigger, I take her very seriously. She is one cold person. She's not even going to go back to check on Tip and Stazi. Her focus is on reuniting me with her boss, using me to convince Grampa Peter to give himself up and then proceed according to the original plan.

The sun is directly overhead now. When I look up at it, I think I see that wide-winged shape again, way far up.

"Hold it," Louise says.

I stop and she comes up to me, kicks one foot behind my ankle, and pulls on my shoulder so that I have to sit down quick or fall. A Canada jay squawks and flaps up and startles Louise. She almost snaps a shot off at it before realizing it's just a small bird. The scent of the patch of wintergreen I've found myself sitting in drifts up to my nose. There's red-capped reindeer moss growing on the side and top of the boulder next to me. I can see the ridges rolling away beyond, and a part of me—even though I know I'm in mortal danger—is thinking how beautiful this all is right now.

But I can see that is not how Louise feels. She's way jumpier than she lets on. She's not at ease or at home here. To her this place is alien and threatening, even if she is armed to the teeth—with her own gun and Tip's, the big bowie knife in the sheath on her belt, smaller buck knife on the other side, and probably a couple of hand grenades or maybe a rocket launcher up her sleeve.

She points up at the sky. "What's going on?" she says. "You know something, don't you? Why no planes?"

She's been paying closer attention than I thought.

"They've been trying to keep flights from going low over the White Mountains," I answer. "So they won't bother the hikers. When planes are way up high, they're hard to see."

All of that is true, even if it isn't the complete answer I could actually give her.

"And what is that big bird we keep seeing?" she says. Her voice is suspicious, but I can tell that she wants to hear something that will reassure her. So I oblige.

"Turkey buzzards look even bigger than eagles. They like to circle way high where the hot air rises."

The truth again. Although I am willing to bet that is no turkey buzzard up there.

Louise looks as if she's about to say something more, but instead she looks at her watch.

"Up," she says. "Darby's waiting."

CHAPTER TWENTY-SEVEN

Onward and Upward

"Ah, the wandering boy has been brought back to us. Callooh callay. The prodigal son returneth. Shall we kill the fatted calf?"

It's only been about three seconds since I came into view of Darby Field posing theatrically on a flat boulder, and I am already sick of his oily voice.

Field unfolds his arms and steps down to grab me by the chin. I don't resist as he turns my head back and forth to get a better look at the blood clotted on my cheeks and in my hair. He shakes his head and then lets go of me.

"Louise," he says in a disappointed voice, "my dear girl, didn't I ask you not to damage the merchandise?"

"He's walking, isn't he?" Louise replies. "Ask him what happened to your boys, Tip and Stazi."

The crocodile grin vanishes from Darby Field's face. His right hand whips out and slaps me so hard across my cheek that it makes a sound like the crack of a gunshot. It spins me halfway around. His other hand grabs me by the wrist and jerks me back toward him. His nostrils flare with anger as he shoves his face so close to me that I can see the red lines of broken blood vessels in the whites of his eyes.

"Where?" he snarls, so angry that his words are almost choking him. "Where . . . are . . . my . . . men?" He holds his hand up to threaten me with another slap.

I don't react. I don't act defiant. I don't stare him in the eyes, daring him to do it again. I just stand there looking down at the ground, so that striking me will give him about as much satisfaction as hitting a dummy.

Field is breathing hard, but my lack of response is not what he expected. He lowers his hand, then repeats his question in a calmer voice, as if rage had never taken him over.

"Where are Tip and Stazi?"

Give an angry man a gift. That's an old proverb Mom taught me. So this time I give him some of what he wants, though I'm careful to word it so it doesn't make me seem that much responsible.

"Tip got all tangled up in some brush while he was chasing me. I was able to sort of tie him up, so he's still stuck there. Stazi slid on some wet rocks, and I think he broke his leg. When he shot at me, I ran away."

Field nods and looks at Louise, who shrugs her shoulders since she didn't go to check on either of his missing henchmen.

"All right," Field says. "We shall retrieve them later. For now—Louise, would you handle the camera?—we shall press on."

Field doesn't ask how I managed to get my hands free. He's too busy composing his next dramatic monologue. He has Louise tie me up again. They're out of duct tape, so this time she uses nylon cord, which would have been cutting into me even more if I hadn't tensed up my muscles and pressed out against the cord after the first time around my wrists. It's one of the Houdini tricks that Grampa Peter taught me. After the person tying you up is done, it looks as if your bindings are tight, but as soon as you relax, they loosen up and there's enough room to start working yourself free.

The fact that she also wrapped the cord around my waist so that my wrists would be tight against my body actually helped too, since she hadn't knotted the cord before she did that. Louise may be good at some things, but tying up captives is apparently Stazi's specialty, not hers.

She is also in a hurry—because Field is waiting impatiently in his arms-folded pose back on the boulder. She quickly gets out the smaller of the two cameras.

"Ready?" Field says.

Louise moves around him, getting different angles as he delivers a speech about how close he is to their forbidden mystery, how even though two of his crew were injured and he wanted to stop and secure immediate medical attention for them, they begged him to press on. Onward and upward (and he makes a heroic flourish with his extended right hand, like Don Quixote lifting up his sword), for his motto is *ad astra per aspera*. To the stars through difficulties.

And I have to listen to this hogwash. Talk about torture!

He signals "Cut," and Louise lowers the camera.

"And now," he says, "after the fox!"

"Which way?" Louise dares to ask. The tone of her voice is sort of insolent now.

"Ah," Field says. He walks a few paces up the trail and then points theatrically at a patch of soft earth. "Behold, O ye of little faith."

Louise pushes me ahead of her, and we both look over Field's shoulder at what he's pointing to. It's a perfect footprint from my grandfather's left boot. Field climbs a little farther, a superior smile on his face, and then points again, this time at a thin piece of torn cloth, the same color of Grampa Peter's shirt. It's tangled in the scraggly branches of a dwarf juniper.

"Elementary, my dear Watson," he intones in his most self-satisfied, superior voice.

He probably thinks he's the great white tracker, like Hawkeye from *The Last of the Mohicans*, finding my grandfather's trail like that. I'm pretty sure Stazi wouldn't make the mistake he's making. But Stazi is not here. I look at Louise out of the corner of my eye, wondering if she'll fall for it too. However, she doesn't say anything.

It's no accident that Grampa Peter, who knows how to disappear without a trace when he wants to, has left those marks.

CHAPTER TWENTY-EIGHT

Mist

We've been climbing for over an hour now and we're well above the tree line, where there's nothing but dwarfed brush and lichen among the stones. It's easy to imagine myself back in the time of the flood, when all life was washed away by the great waters that came just shy of the top of this mountain.

I'm not talking about the Bible story, but our own ancient tale. Long, long ago the people were out of balance. They showed no respect for the earth. Instead of hunting for food and clothing, they killed things for pleasure. Instead of picking berries, they pulled the bushes up by the roots. When they fished, they would catch every fish in the stream with nets and leave most of them to rot on the shore.

Only the people of one small village remembered to do things the right way, to give thanks and to only take what they needed. In fact, they went out of their way to be kind. One day, a man and woman from that little village saw a rabbit that had fallen in the river and was about to drown. They pulled that rabbit out and set him free out of the kindness of their hearts.

But most of the people continued hurting everything around then. Finally, Ktsi Nwaskw, the Great Mystery, sent a flood to cleanse the earth of those bad people. Of course the Great Mystery warned the animal and bird and insect nations first and provided ways for them to survive. The flood was only meant to wipe out human beings.

The rabbit, though, took pity on the people of the little village. He went to that man and woman who had saved him and told them a flood was coming.

"Follow me," the rabbit said. Then, with the waters rising behind them, he led that couple and the other people of the village up to the very top of Agiocochook, where the flood could not drown them.

That is why, to this day, we incise the shape of the rabbit onto birch bark and carve it into wood. We want to remember how that rabbit saved us and how important it is to show respect to all things in creation.

It's not a story that the people who are dragging me up the mountain would understand. As far as they are concerned, the most important thing in life is to get as much for yourself as you possibly can.

"We have your grandson!" Darby Field yells, his hands cupped around his mouth. It is maybe the twentieth time he has yelled this as we've been following Grampa Peter's trail. I keep waiting for Field and Louise to wise up that they're being led the way he wants them to go. But I guess their greed has made them blind, blind to the fact, too, that a wall of mist has been following us up the mountain as we've climbed.

Why can't they see, as I can, that we are being pushed up the mountain by that wall of mist? We're not being followed by floodwaters, but something just as powerful and deadly is waiting above us at the highest point.

Suddenly my grandfather appears right in front of us. It isn't as if he stepped out from behind a stone or stood up from some hiding place. One moment he was not there and in the next breath he was.

Darby Field lets out a noise like a toad that's been stepped on and jumps back. Louise is probably equally surprised, but keeps her cool and stares hard at Grampa Peter, who holds out both his hands, palms up.

"Here," he says.

And what he means is, I give myself up to you. I am going to give you what you want.

His eyes make contact with mine, and I get the message as he flicks his gaze behind me. I'm to hold back, wait for the right moment, and be very cautious. I understand that last bit from the expression on his face. It's not fear, but the look of someone who has just seen something that made his heart pound. And he seems tired, as if what he has just done—and it's not the quick climb to the top—has taken much of his energy. I think again about where we are on this trail into the past.

I try to go to his side. Louise grabs the line around my waist and yanks me back behind her.

"Stay," she commands me. Apparently she and Darby Field both learned their people skills at the same dog obedience school. She points one of her guns at Grampa Peter and gestures up with it. "Lead the way, gramps."

Field gives her a fishy glare. He wanted to be the one to take control, especially after embarrassing himself with that toad squawk. But Grampa Peter has already started climbing, mist swirling about him. The clouds are all around us.

Now I see things I recognize. Formations of stone, the way the path sweeps in and out of them. We are almost at the very top of Agiocochook. It has gotten much cooler, and not just from the mist, which blocks out the view in all directions.

There's a strange tension in the air, though I seem to be the only one who notices it. And there's a faint scent that I think I've smelled before. We just passed over the place where the road was cut up the mountain decades ago. But there's no road here. No cog railway, no weather station, no human-built structures.

Something else, though, is here. I know that Grampa Peter feels its presence as much as I do. I only hope that it knows the difference between our intentions and those of the man and woman with us.

Grampa Peter looks back over his shoulder. We're in a tight group now, the only way we can all keep each other in sight. No one is more than an arm's length apart.

"Here!" he says, dropping his arms. At the same

172

time he cuts his eyes quickly to the left. Then he takes a quick step to the right and vanishes.

Things begin to happen fast. I yank free of Louise's grasp, turn, dive into the mist, and begin to run down the slope. I think I know where I'm going, but a rock turns under my foot and I find myself twisting to the side and going down on my right knee.

Good thing, too. I hear the blast of Louise's gun from behind me and feel a searing pain as the bullet tears through my jacket and the flesh of my left shoulder. She's firing blind, but I know that shot was meant for the back of my head.

I crawl forward as more shots ricochet off the stones. Then I'm around a rock, and up on my feet. My knee is numb, and all I can do right now is limp, not run. There's a wind in my face that wasn't blowing before. It is cutting through the mist that hid me, sweeping it off the mountain. They'll be able to see me and get off a shot at me if I don't find a place to hide.

A strangled cry comes from up the mountain. And though I probably shouldn't look back, I can't help myself. The wind has cut a path through the clouds and I can see the peak fifty feet away from me perfectly. Field and Louise have fallen to the ground and are looking up at the tall dark figure above them, its wide black wings spread, blotting out the setting sun. Its pitiless gaze is on them. Then, as if feeling my eyes on it, it turns its head in my direction.

I whirl around, start to run. I'm not limping anymore. If there is one place on earth I shouldn't be right now, this is it!

CHAPTER TWENTY-NINE

The Cave

It's dark now. Eerily so. I suppose I've been on my own for at least an hour. But I can't tell what time it is because my watch is no longer working. Maybe it broke when I hit it against the rocks. I've lost the trail several times and have had to turn and slowly feel my way back to it. At least my trick of flexing against my bonds as I was tied up served its purpose. I was able to work myself free—not as fast as a professional escape artist, but quick enough to avoid too many out-of-control falls.

There's no light from the sky, no sign of moon or stars. I've never been afraid of the dark, but right now I am definitely wary of what it's hiding. I've thought more than once of taking out my Mini Maglite, which is still zipped into the inner pocket of my jacket. But showing a light in enemy territory is one of the worst mistakes a soldier can make, according to Mom. The beam might show me a few feet of the path, but it could also show someone—something—where I am. Most people are so scared of the dark that the first thing they do is try to make a light.

I don't say its name, not even in my thoughts. Grampa Peter has told me more than once to be careful about that. Do not say or think the name of anything with power, unless you want it to be heard. If you are in rattlesnake territory, you never say or think the word *rattlesnake*, because doing that might call it to you. If you have to mention it to someone else, maybe to warn them that there are dangerous reptiles around, you should say something like, "Watch out for a moving stick." Words have power, and names have even more power. So I don't allow the name of that old being to come into my mind.

I just keep moving, and if my mind starts to stray I count my steps. I'm up to a thousand and twenty now.

It's quiet all around me. Ever since I started to run it's been quiet, except for the rattle of stones dislodged by my clumsy feet. The last loud noises I heard were three loud cries from behind and above me. Not shouts of terror and despair, like the one that burst from Darby Field and led me to turn and see the scene that made the hair stand up on the back of my neck. Those three harsh, echoing cries that split the air came from no human throat.

One thousand and forty, one thousand and forty-one . . .

Actually, it hasn't been completely quiet. Twice when I've paused, I've thought I heard something. A soft sound that came not from behind or in front of me, but from high above. Almost like the sound of a kite flapping in the wind or a sheet hung on the line, buffeted by a breeze. Or—and I don't want to think this, which is why I only allow it to come to me as a last comparison—like wide wings in the night.

The thought of that makes me start to walk faster.

Onethousandfiftyone, onethousandfiftytwo, one thou—dang!

I've run into another rock with my knee. I can't keep going like this. I have to stop, try to get my bearings. Breathe. That's what both Mom and Dad would tell me to do in a situation like this. If you run in panic, you may end up running toward whatever danger panicked you.

I sit down and take a slow breath. As soon as I do that, the sky begins to clear over me, and the moon shows itself. It lights not just the path and the roll of ridges visible from this high place, but a narrow dark opening in the rock face right next to me. A cave. One I've never seen before.

Then I hear something. Wide leathery wings. I'm sure of it. The sound is not high in the sky. It's coming closer, toward me. I look up. A black shape is dropping down from above me, blotting out the moon.

I duck my head and leap frantically for the cave mouth, just as something strikes at me. A talon digs into my wounded shoulder, tearing my jacket even more. I twist away, claw into the cave, pulling my legs in just before something hits the stones hard. I'm panting, as winded as if I just ran ten miles. I turn around and see the glint of red eyes staring at me from outside. A low throaty growl, then a long arm reaches in, clawed fingers spread wide. I scuttle back as quickly as I can, praying that it is too big to force its way in after me.

The cave is wider back here, the roof higher. It's so dark that I can't see anything, but I can hear a soft fluttering sound from above me. Little brown bats, most likely. Caves like this are their home at this time of year. Bats don't bother me at all. Plus worrying about creatures with little wings is the last thing on my mind now.

I take a deep breath, trying to slow my pounding heart before it explodes in my chest like a grenade. The faint light of the moon shining through the narrow opening ten yards away, no longer blocked by a huge body. Has it given up? Not likely.

I crawl farther back to look for another way out of here. I reach in front of me to keep from banging into anything. Good thing, too, because my hand finds a wall in front of me, walls and roof narrowing in on each side. I've reached the end of the cave.

I'm trapped.

CHAPTER THIRTY

The Light

Someone once asked Grampa Peter if he ever got lost in the mountains. His reply was simple: "Nope."

But if that person had asked Grampa Peter to clarify that answer some, Grampa Peter might have added what he later said to me: "But I got confused one time for about two weeks."

His real point was that you are never lost until you think you are. It's just that some times are harder than others when it comes to finding your way.

I'm remembering that right now. Being trapped is like being lost, I think. But am I really trapped?

I begin to feel my way along the wall in front of me. There's a draft of air coming from somewhere. I reach down and find a place just above the floor where there is space between the stones.

The caves in these mountains are made by great slabs of stone that have slid down, piled on top of one another. So I'm not surprised to find this place where the rocks don't fit neatly together. It's too small to squeeze through, but it's probably big enough to see through.

I get out my flashlight and press the button. The beam that shoots out of it is so intense that it hurts my eyes after all this darkness. I blink, then gradually open my eyes, letting them get used to seeing light again. I fasten the Velcro strap around my head, crouch down, stick the light into the crevice, and put my cheek against the stone so I can see through with one eye. And what I see makes me gasp.

It's a much larger chamber than this one. I can't tell exactly how big it is, but I can't see the walls on either side. In the middle is what looks to be a big sleeping mat, maybe ten feet across. It's made of evergreen boughs woven together, the way we sometimes cover the floor of a lean-to when we're out in the forest for a few nights and need to make a quick, comfortable shelter. Some of the boughs are so fresh that they are still green. My nose picks up the scent of crushed balsam needles, and I see that the sleeping nest is dented in the center like someone—something—big has been resting there.

But I only glance at that briefly because as I move my narrow flashlight beam about, it reflects off hundreds of points of light. Objects that glitter and gleam. I know what I am seeing. It's Pmola's treasure.

I can't help myself. I start chuckling. But it's bitter laughter at the thought of all Grampa Peter and I have been put through. Tears are coming to my eyes as I laugh, thinking of the things Darby Field and his crew have done to others in search of wealth that, compared to human lives, is always really worthless in the long run. All the nervous energy that's been bottled up in me is coming out.

I focus light once more on Pmola's great treasure. Precious objects all right, things that my ancestors saw as full of power and meaning, but far from the riches that modern people covet.

Not silver or gold, not diamonds or rubies. Instead what I see are carefully piled stacks of quartz crystals, shiny stones that contain iron pyrite—fool's gold—and some roughly made bracelets that might be pounded copper. All brought there by Pmola over who knows how many years, how many centuries, the way a crow will pick up something shiny and carry it back to its nest.

How many centuries? Thinking of that long passage of time reminds me of where I am. I'm in that other time, the time of our old stories. How would my ancestors have related to this? What would they have done if they found themselves where I am? What could they have said—and in what tongue? And how would Grampa Peter behave?

I lean back from the crevice, turn my flashlight beam back the way I came. I've seen the light now. I know what I need to do.

I start making my way back to the cave entrance, thinking about the right words to use. I pause at the cave mouth and turn my light off. The moon's bright enough to cast a faint shadow on the ground. Sometimes moon shadows are really exaggerated, but I know that the very large shadow I am seeing reflects the shape that is waiting out there, a wide-winged shape on top of a great boulder, the shadow widening and narrowing as those leathery wings open and close.

Breathe. I crawl out through the cave mouth slowly. Fast movements always attract night hunters. I feel Pmola's cold gaze on the back of my neck and I turn around.

It's right there, not more than an arm's length from me, so close that I can see the ripple of the muscles under its sleek black pelt as it raises one arm. Pmola seems as big as the mountain itself.

Like most Abenaki kids of my generation, I was not raised with just our old language. Instead, what I heard most of the time was English with a few words and phrases in Indian mixed in. I've always wished I could speak our language as well as Grampa Peter, but at least I know some of the most important words. And right now I know that anything I say should be in our old tongue. And I think I know what those words should be: the phrase that we all speak to each other at the start of the new year when we want to begin fresh with clear minds and forgiving hearts.

I don't look up into Pmola's dark eyes. That might be seen as a challenge. Instead I look down at the earth, bow my head to show my respect, and speak.

"Anhaldam mawi kassipalilawalan." Forgive me for any wrong I may have done to you.

I can hear the even rhythm of Pmola's breath from at least five feet over my head. Then a sound I didn't expect.

"Hmmph!"

Is there approval in that sound? I risk looking up and see that Pmola is holding out its long arm and pointing with one razor-clawed finger toward a trail that leads down the mountain.

"Go," Pmola says in a voice that reverberates through me like the clang of a huge bell.

I hesitate, though. I wasn't just asking for understanding and forgiveness for myself, but also for Grampa Peter. I don't know where he is or what's happened to him. I can't leave the mountain without him. But how can I tell that to a creature that could take off my head with one swipe of its claw?

"Piel!" a voice calls to me from down the trail that Pmola just pointed to. It's Grampa Peter. Even in the moonlight I recognize his familiar shape. He's gesturing to me with an open hand.

I take one step backward and then another. The huge, black-winged being stands there as still as a statue, although it does seem as if the expression on its long-muzzled face has changed just the slightest bit. I might be wrong, but it almost looks amused. Then I turn and walk forward to take my grandfather's outstretched hand. We go down the mountain together. We don't say anything and we don't look back.

At first we pass through a thick curtain of mist. Then the way ahead of us begins to clear. We stay silent and walk on as minutes and then hours pass.

There is more light around us even though the moon is gone. It's the first light that comes before dawn. I'm concentrating on the trail because it is starting to look familiar. There's a pond, as green as emerald at the foot of a cascade. Gem Pond. I know where we are. Less than half a mile later we cross a brook. We're on the Ammonoosuc Ravine Trail that leads to the parking lot on the Base Road.

Birds are singing to greet the new day, and I hear the sound of human voices as well. Around the bend, climbing up toward us is a party of five or six hikers getting an early start.

As we pass, they hardly give us a second glance. Hands raised, they greet us as if we are nothing out of the ordinary, even though neither of us has a pack and my torn clothes and the bloodstains on my coat must make me look as if I've been wrestling with a bear. They're totally focused on the climb ahead of them.

"Hi!"

"Great day for a hike."

"Yo."

I smile and say hi to each of them in turn.

When they are all past, I look at Grampa Peter. He nods at me. We're back in our own time again.

It is midmorning when we reach the parking lot. I suddenly feel as if I'm about to collapse. My legs are shaking.

"Here," Grampa Peter says. He helps me sit down. Then he walks over to a Land Rover with out-of-state plates. Its middle-aged owners look friendly and also unlikely to do anything more than turn around and drive back down the road after having come this far.

"My grandson had a bad fall," he says. "Lost his pack. Could you give us a ride down the mountain?"

It's one of the longest speeches I have ever heard him make, and it works. Fred and Irma Peck turn out to be two of the kindest folks you could ever want to meet, visiting New Hampshire from Indiana to see the Presidentials. They've got a thermos full of something they call sweet tea and they insist that I drink some of it and eat one of the energy bars they've got in their glove box.

"We're taking you two right to your door," Irma says as she hands me a second energy bar. "It's only a little out of our way."

"Not every day we get a chance to be Good Samaritans," Fred adds with a big grin.

"Thank you both so much," I keep saying in between sips of tea and mouthfuls of carob-covered caramel and nuts.

"Why, son," Irma says, "it's nothing more than anyone would do if they had a chance."

Ironically, she says that just as we go past the place where Darby Field turned off the road. Was that only a day and a half ago? I look over at Grampa Peter, who I'm sure is thinking just what I am.

No, there are some people in the world who would not do what the good-hearted Pecks are doing. Far from it.

CHAPTER THIRTY-ONE

Surviving the Hardships

Two months have passed since Grampa Peter and I came down from Agiocochook. I start school tomorrow and I am sort of looking forward to it. After years of saying no to coaches, I've finally decided to try out for the basketball team. It turns out I can shoot the ball better than I thought.

One morning, after the wound in my shoulder healed up, Grampa Peter pulled up with a backboard and a hoop in the back of his truck.

"Exercise therapy," he said. Then he tossed

me a new red-and-black basketball, and the two of us set up a half-court on the paved drive in front of the trailer.

My first left-handed shot swished through the net without touching the rim. I just about couldn't miss when I shot from that side, whether it was a fall-away or an actual dunk.

Maybe it's that the rest of my body has finally caught up with all the height I put on over the last two years. I've been filling out more, too, adding muscle. I'm twenty pounds heavier than at the start of the summer, and none of it is fat.

Or maybe there's another reason why I healed up so fast. Why I've been getting stronger. Why I have such accuracy when I shoot a basketball. Why I have so much more self-confidence. Maybe when Pmola touched me with its talon, it wasn't trying to hurt me. Maybe it was actually giving me a gift, like it gave that hunter in Dad's story.

There are times when I wake up in the morning and wonder if what happened to us was just a dream. But I know it wasn't. It's just like when I wake up thinking that Mom and Dad are in the next room and not off in Iraq. Some things that you wish were just unpleasant dreams are real. Life is hard a lot of the time. The trick, as Mom said to me once, is not to expect things to get easier. Just get better at surviving the hardships.

I open my email. Nothing new today from Mom or Dad yet, but I have to remember that time in the Middle East is different. When it's day here, it's night there. In more ways than one. But I hear from them regularly. They're both doing okay. They've sent me loads of photos. My favorite, which I printed out and stuck to the wall above my bed, shows them with their faces so close together that they are cheek to cheek, smiling so wide that it looks like one big grin between the two of them.

They're going to be all right. I know that in my heart. And when I said that to Grampa Peter, that my parents were going to come home safe and sound, he looked at me like he was looking into me. Then he nodded in a way that told me a lot of things.

Grampa Peter and I have exchanged knowing looks a few times over the last week when we've tuned in to cable's *The Search for Darby Field: Mystery Man's Mysterious Disappearance.* Apparently no one noticed that his group was missing until weeks after Grampa Peter and I last saw them. It seems that Field always kept a cloak of secrecy over his movements. Even his producer had no idea where exactly Field had been heading when he left Boston. All he knew was that it was somewhere in New England. Grampa Peter and I are the only ones who know where they really were when the past, literally, caught up with them.

A week into the search a local news anchor and cameraman tried to interview Grampa Peter, seeing as how he was the Native American elder who knew the most about these mountains, which might have been Field's destination.

Although news shows these days like short sound bites, Grampa's usual "yups" and "nopes" were a little too short for that news anchor. She gave up on the interview after ten minutes.

Did the four of them survive? Are Field and his crew alive and caught in the past? I have to admit, I'm not worried about them. All I know is that wherever they are, it's better than having them here among us.

I lean back in my chair and close my eyes. I see a tourist who has parked his car on Base Road to take a picture. It's ten, maybe twenty years from now. He notices an old trail that was concealed by the slope of the road, climbs down to follow it—ten yards, twenty, a hundred—as it turns and twists away from the road. He sees a glint of rusting metal, pushes aside a branch, and sees a van deep in the evergreen thicket. He reads the fading words on the van's side. Then he sees that a trail begins just past that spruce thicket and thinks of taking it.

But just as he has that thought, he realizes the day is fading, the sun slipping behind the western slopes. He hears a sound from overhead, something like the beating of wide wings. He looks up, but doesn't see anything. Still, by the time he reaches the familiar safety of the highway above him, clawing his way up the slope in panic, he's deeply relieved to see that nothing has followed him. He stands there, breathing hard. His heart is pounding.

Why was that van with its strange name hidden down there? What happened to those who left it?

That hiker will never be able to imagine just how strange the answers to those questions really are.

JOSEPH BRUCHAC

is the author of SKELETON MAN, THE RETURN OF SKELETON MAN, BEARWALKER, THE DARK POND, and WHISPER IN THE DARK as well as numerous other critically acclaimed novels, poems, and stories, many drawing on his Abenaki heritage. Mr. Bruchac and his wife, Carol, live in upstate New York, in the same house where he was raised by his grandparents. You can visit him online at www.josephbruchac.com.